MW01230553

JAMES FISHER

Spiritcrusher's Crusade Volume II: Flesh Cabal

For my girls—the only light remaining in a dark world.

Stay strong, but hold on tight. Spirit Crusher-

DEATH, "SPIRIT CRUSHER"

Contents

Preface

Reader, the contents of this novel are not for the faint of heart. Within the pages of this macabre work, many unsavory (and downright vile) events occur. Here's your fucking trigger list.

- Torture
- Cannibalism
- Dismemberment
- Sexual Assault
- Pedophilia/SA on children/infants
- Mass Murder
- Drugging
- Abduction
- Human Trafficking
- Insects

Acknowledgement

I would like to thank a few very important people, without whom this book would not exist. Your friendship and opinions mean the world to me.

Veronica- who edited, alpha/beta read, and is crucial to this story. Despite all the chaos of life, you never shied away from helping me. Thank you.

Post-Mortem- who designed my wrap, among teaching me many things I'd neglected before. A great friend, fan, and supporter. Your knowledge and enthusiasm is invaluable.

Thank you both. Your friendship keeps me afloat when times get dark.

I: Unfinished Business With Vince

I am Spiritcrusher, and this is my crusade.

My revelation had left me depressed, forlorn and with an aching need to rectify mistakes that were simply too far gone. Visions of children being headshot or mauled by hammer and baton branded themselves deep into my subconscious. Asimov had been tending to Vince Lauris in the kill room the past two days while I desperately tried to get a grip. At times, the exercise felt like one of futility.

Getting cold feet was completely out of the question in my line of work. Shit or get off the pot, as they say. No time like the present. Saying to move your ass is one thing, getting up to do it another entirely. I begrudgingly rose to relieve myself on the third day at around noon.

Allen's gentle and overly cautious laughter drifted up softly from the kitchen where Asy had been giving him cooking lessons. This was not an idea proposed by myself. Apparently, the kid loved cooking—and according to our android friend— he was *damn* good at it. Tack that onto his already impressive knack for painting, and I found I had a prodigy in my hands.

In the mirror, my nude form bore scars from a lifetime of

servitude to a malevolent deity. Gunshot wounds healed over into pink rings dotted my chest and abdomen, my skin pale and eyes bloodshot. Admittedly, some of the current visible wear upon my face was of my doing. Since seeing the footage of myself in the hallway, I'd been drinking bourbon and snorting copious rails of cocaine. Nothing abated the pain.

I relieved myself, giving that beautiful fat cock a fair shake. Unsurprisingly, it responded with a friendly surge of blood and heat. Instead of humoring my reawakened libido, I washed my hands and went over the course of actions for the day. This was one session I wasn't eager for—because I needed to keep that cunt alive long enough to eke out some useful intel.

Needless to say, the fat fuck would be a heap of ash by now if he didn't serve a greater purpose other than sheer slaughter. This pedophile organization was a sea of interconnecting businesses—some media, some law enforcement, and a slew of gun-toting cronies and snuff making scum. Given the scraps of information I already possessed, it was a wretched cabal of flesh peddlers, the likes of which the world had never before seen. If I could just torture him long enough, he would break. They always break. Then I'd have an 'in'—-a way to disassemble the machine that I had raged against for far too long.

I walked over to the shower stall of the all black bathroom, turning the faucet on and letting it grow hot. After hopping in, I efficiently lathered myself with a tea tree oil body wash, quickly getting all the 'hot spots' for odor and bacteria. Hygiene was an important way to jump-start my day and get my mind on an even keel. I may be a serial killer, but I'm not a monster. If my dick ever stinks, may it be because I'm feeding the worms.

After finishing up my basic training-style shower, I quickly donned my black fatigues and tungsten-enforced boots. I paused and took a moment to towel off my hair before combing it back. Even if it was a lie, I had to tell myself things could get better. Looking at the man in the mirror eye-to-eye tore my delicate illusions asunder.

How could anything get better if a dead-eyed monster like me was at the helm of the movement? It was all a fucking joke, a sick mockery of order. But there I was—at the precipice of a new era for vigilante justice—and with nowhere to go but forward. I picked up my black and smooth mask from the bathroom counter, eyeing it as I ran my fingers across its sleek gadgetry.

It had only been two days, but already I could feel the void where my Inner Daemon dwelled, wailing out in unfettered rage. I needed to become the true me. Only by donning an avatar of vicious butchery could I attain completion. With a rapidly rising pulse—I let my true face slide downwards—concealing the lie my maker handed me in dismissive contempt.

Spiritcrusher walked out of the bedroom, Leon checked into a small box until he'd be useful. I went downstairs, turning towards the left wing. On the right, I could hear my only friends enjoying the culinary lessons. Despite everything that happened or what was yet to come, I smiled. Black and red Damascus walls covered in art slipped by as I walked to the end of the hall.

I entered a passcode into a number-pad for the automated door system. It beeped, and the door slid left as I made my way downstairs to the place where dreams come true. My dreams, that is. For my captives, it was a nightmare from which they never woke. My booted feet's heavy footfalls echoed down the stairwell, and I savored the tension I could feel from my honored guest in the depths of my dungeon.

"Good afternoon, cupcake," I said jauntily as I strolled in. Vince was in a state, to say the least. His formerly coiffed dark hair was disheveled and oily, his face bruised and skin a sallow hue. Worst of all, his poor little baby-dick was now null. Asy tried to save it, but the railroad spike sounding rod/jump-start combo was simply too much damage to rectify. Not that I had any regrets, of course. I'd do it again forty times a day for all eternity, and not lose a wink of sleep.

"Just—kill—me," he croaked hoarsely. He had been screaming again. I chuckled, walking up to him and shoving my fist into his mouth abruptly. Vince's eyes bulged and his face grew red. Ripples of jiggling fat rolled across his vibrating form as he struggled to breathe.

"You've been calling for help, pumpkin? Have you not learned *anything?*"

I withdrew my fist, and he coughed, spluttering for air as his color slowly returned to normal. I slung beads of his spit from my hand onto the floor, feeling a tidal wave of revulsion. Never before had I wanted torture to just be fucking *over.*

"This entire place is sound-proofed, you daft twat. Did you *really* think crying for help would work?" Vince eyed me loathingly, working his sore jaw. I didn't want his feedback, anyway. This was my moment to emphasize urgency.

"I swear, you must be fucking delusional. After *all* those families you've torn apart—all those snuff films produced under your leadership—and you think there's some higher being who'll protect you? *Save YOU?!*" I snarled. His eyes widened in open fear. I continued on my verbal tirade—a soapbox lecture held for a nude pedophile strapped to a torture chair.

"No, my little rodent. Here, *I* am your god. *I* decide when the pain stops in this physical realm. Two days of recovery, and you're already getting wild-eyed notions of escape or rescue. I had hoped someone running an ops location would be a mite more intelligent. Oh well. Break's over."

Vince instantly shook his head side-to-side, panicking at whatever I had in store for him. As always, I just winged it. Why plot out every little beat? It's so much more fun to improvise and see how things shake out. "No, no. Please. Please. What do you want?! Anything!!" he cried desperately. I tutted him and walked over to a steel control panel on the far wall. There was my trusty incinerator button, but there was also a button for adjusting the chair's configuration. I pressed the latter.

The chair flattened underneath him, shifting into more of a steel gurney, the straps automatically tightening. Then, the foot of the steel slab elevated slowly, leaving Vince at an even more compromising position. "Please, do no more. I'll do whatever you say, I swear!" I laughed softly. "Shut the fuck up and get ready."

I unfastened my fly buttons, pulling out my cock and letting it cast a wide shadow on his greasy little rat face. In that moment, I was a Hellish monolith over one soul of millions to suffer. I sighed, and let the fresh torrent of piss flow. Vince coughed and blustered as I waterboarded him with my ammonia-rich supply.

I urinated until there was none left, leaving him hacking and retching with his feet in the air.

"So, where can I access the master list of locations, Vince? Tell me quickly, because I intend to continue waterboarding you if you don't. And I'm out of piss. So it won't be good."

He hacked, and it was apparent by his reaction that he didn't want a diarrhea waterboard. Honestly, *I* didn't want to do it, either. There are some smells that don't wash out, no matter how many passes Asimov makes. "I'm waiting," I said impatiently.

"I—I don't know about that *myself*, but I *do* know the Unit that runs technological processes for the—company." My eyebrow raised in interest at this. For as many heads as I'd cracked, this was the most substantial intel I'd gathered. I blame my high mortality rate. "Okay, I'm listening. What's the company name?"

He paused for a moment, and I could see the gears turning in his mind. I hoped he'd have enough sense to know that there's no going back once you let a crumb of information slip to the enemy. Quickly, I grew impatient. "NOW. Or you get waterboarded with shit. I've been on a coke and bourbon bender. You do *not* want a throat full of what I'll be shitting out."

"The—the company name is—Precious Cargo Productions," he said in a fearful voice. I stopped dead in my tracks, the company name a lightning bolt of disgust striking me at my core. The Daemon was just on the other side of the veil, his claws scratching at the delicate barrier, begging for sweet freedom. With a great degree of restraint, I cast aside my need to kill. I was so close to having enough to work with. So fucking close to sending this pile of moldy shit to Hell.

"Good boy. That's a start. Where's the tech center? Be quick about it, I don't have any residual patience after the week I've had." I stared Vince down, relishing the little moment-by-moment intricacies of him weighing his very limited options. It didn't take him long to see there was only one way out of his plight. Surrender. Surrender and death.

"It's Unit 403-7, in Atlanta. Please, let me go. I've told you everything I know. I'm not the show runner here, man. I'm just mid-level management. If—"

I kneed Vince in his pathetic face hard, blood flowing like a faucet from his crunched-in cartilage. He squirmed and screamed dumbly at the strike.

"You're not going anywhere, idiot. All you've done is prevent me from shitting down your throat. I saved something for you from your suite in 378-6. Don't go anywhere—oh, *that's* right. You fucking can't." I belly-laughed as I walked out of the suite with his miserable pleas trailing behind.

I grabbed the tool for Vince's grand finale from my armory on the second floor, then paged Asimov over my watch. By the time I reached the bottom of the carpeted grand stairwell, my android friend was there waiting dutifully. Asy was a sleekly humanoid robot, his eyes glowing blue rings and motions strangely fluid. "Master Leon, it's good to see you up and about. How might I serve you, sir?"

"Good man. Thanks. Get big boy down there in the position. I've got an idea for a good show."

II: Pegged

By the time I had returned to the kill room, Vince's beaten up ass was on display. Asimov had hog-tied him and positioned him on the table. Lights were aimed at the subject—that subject being an ass about to get hate fucked with a strap-on. Nails had been driven through the dildo all the way from tip to base. "Time to get a taste of your own medicine, you pathetic little fuck-pig."

"No, no, no!" he shrieked like some naked and deformed goblin—utterly pathetic.

I whistled gaily, strolling over to the camera to ensure the frame had been properly set. It had. Asy was wonderful at every task I inquired of him. No time like the present. Shit or get off the pot.

I put the harness on my hips and secured the crucified dildo onto it by slotting it into position. As I tightened all the proper straps, I took a slight moment to appreciate the amount of work lesbians and peggers go through to do what they enjoy. Maybe there's some kindness out in the world, after all. Everything was ready.

Standing behind Vince, I could feel his fear. It radiated off of him, made the room have a sickly sweet stench. His asshole was puckered and dark, hair running the entire trench between his ass cheeks. I spit on the strap-on, aligning it with my target.

When the tip rested against his hole, he pleaded more. I didn't have the energy to talk anymore. So, I rammed it in. Nails gouged out long lines of flesh as the hate-dildo jammed halfway inside of him. Blood poured like a spigot. I'd tapped into a whole different kind of crude.

With each thrust, the plastic cock begrudgingly jammed itself deeper into his dark inner-workings. Blood and shit flowed around it, drenching my pants and the floor. It only made me hate him more. I grabbed his love handles and slammed it to the base as he screamed and spasmed like he was having a seizure.

The dildo slowly loosened its grip as I pummeled the pedophile's flabby ass. I heard a ripping sound somewhere inside of him, and I couldn't help but look down at it as I pulled out for another in-thrust. Intestines had raveled themselves around the nails, not unlike a fork twirling spaghetti. I thrust it back in, and as I rhythmically pumped his disintegrating o-ring, the resistance of his dirt-channel lost its grip.

By the time I stopped, Vince had passed out, his insides hanging from his ass. What was once a bog-standard middle-aged man's ass(hemorrhoids, dingleberries, that sort of thing), was now a gaping crimson portal to a dimension of shit. Simply put, I had bored a six-inch diameter chasm into his digestive tract and left it in ruins. Gastric juices and feces hung heavy in the air, little nuggets of dung splatting on the table around Vince as blood ebbed and flowed from his ruined boypussy.

"Shame you're passed out, cunt. But I got what I've been looking for, and let's face facts—you were never going to turn your life around. Dogs get put down," I said, releasing the harness with a quick yanking motion. I walked over to the table, grabbing a chainsaw from the ever-evolving arsenal.

With one good pull, the saw roared to life, diamond-tipped teeth blurring as the scent of burning gasoline overpowered the hanging stench of demolished digestive system. I walked over cautiously, mindful of the blood pooling on the floor. If he had been conscious, the screams of man and machine would have battled it out right there in the kill room. But he was out, going the way of the coward. In silent defeat.

"So—ham or steak?" I asked the passed-out prey. With his looming death, I could feel my spirits rising. I'd never waste time again. Eyeing the pasty pussy, I took a moment to settle on where to hack first. Ham it was. I revved the chainsaw engine to a roar and pressed the teeth into his lower back, just above the ass. With a grunt, I forced it downwards, bone crunching and flesh shredding from the cruel bite. Blood flew in a macabre work of art, the pelvis separating from his torso and spine with a wet thud.

What nail skewers did not yank out before slowly oozed from Vince's separated bottom-half. Intestinal chunks crept out, excrement and blackened blood leaking and congealing like sadistic jelly. I took the chainsaw to the center of his hips, separating his legs, then bisecting them at the knees. Without a care in the world, I tossed the butchered half down, each heavy limb splatting onto the blood-soaked floor and producing a merry splash.

My clothes were drenched in his iron-laden flow, and though I knew my prey had already died, my Daemon wanted more. He was insatiable. I took the chainsaw to his shoulders, removing arms and bisecting them before tossing them onto the heap. Though my Daemon was in full control, a wonderful strategic play came to mind as I continued butchering Vince's still-warm carcass.

I beheaded the corpse, setting it aside before fighting the chainsaw blade through his torso. After five minutes, what was once a 'man' was now a midden heap of disparate body parts. I stood there, letting the violence of the room soak into me. Feed me. Restore me. Empower me.

Now that he was out of the equation, perhaps I'd find a way to strategize again. I couldn't stand around feeling sorry for myself over what became of the children on the top floor of 378-6. It would be far too easy to simply bury the barrel of a .45 in my mouth and vacate my mortal coil. Allen deserved more. The children still in cages deserved more, too.

You're not done, little Leon. I run the shots. Remember?

"Y—yes. I remember," I said obediently to the Daemon.

Good. It's good that you remember. I'd hate for you to—lose control. Hahahahahaha—grab the head. Satiate your dark master.

Inside I felt frozen, helpless. He didn't take full control often. I knew he *really* wanted me to do this. Needed me to. I lifted Vince's severed head, awaiting further instructions.

Fuck his mouth until your testicles are drained.

There was nothing that could be said or done to prevent it. My Daemon held absolute control over me. Without him, I'd never have escaped Richa—

What was that? Trying to remember things? Weren't you just given a clear and actionable order? Should we go upstairs and fuck a different severed head? I can—

"NO!!!"

I stood frozen in existential dread. The time for calling bluffs had gone by long before. I begrudgingly pulled my cock back out, setting the head onto the table. A few skillful strokes, and my dick stood proudly, flush with blood.

Feed him your dick.

Cold, stiff lips offered poor protest as I slid my glans into Vince's mouth and began to slowly pump. His tongue—though dead and stiffened—felt amazing as it massaged my undershaft. I fucked harder, clutching the head aloft by a fistful of hair. Teeth tickled my thick shaft as I pounded the postmortem oral chamber passionately.

I needed this.

I always know what you need.

"Yes—you do, Master. I'm sorry for my impertinence."

Cum was just a stroke away. I roared, pummeling the head until teeth crunched from my force. Gushing waves of pleasure coursed through my throbbing dick. I poured my seed into his dead gullet, fucking to eke out every last drop. It felt so fucking good.

Looking down, I could see my cum pouring in thick waves out the bottom of his neck. It intermingled with blood, giving it the appearance of strawberry shortcake filling. I pulled out of his mouth, setting the head back down for Asy to preserve. It could serve more use in the future.

III: Dinnertime Conversation

Another shower was required after the bloodbath that had transpired in the kill room. My fatigues were soaked through, sticking to my skin. The tang of iron hung heavily in my nostrils. I walked to the grand stairwell, pausing to take in the sounds of Allen and Asimov in the kitchen.

They were wrapping up, given the sounds of dishes being washed. Allen's words were indistinguishable, but his tone carried a note of joy that simply hadn't been there three days before. Despite all the blackened thoughts and pain wracking my soul, the sound brought a smile to my face. I decided then to make the most of the evening.

* * *

Showering was another quick affair, though the moments seemed to expand themselves to eternity. I found myself disassociating as the blood swirled down the drain. It bore the resemblance of a crimson hurricane, spiraling into the dark depths of pipes. Pipes that led to sewers clogged with human waste and not a few bloated corpses. I snapped back to full sentience, lathering up and rinsing off quickly.

The symptoms of my sickness had always been there. I supposed the distinction now was that a child's safety hung directly in my hands now. Allen was the key to a better life, a better world. All bets hinged upon his safety, his comfort.

I stepped out of the shower as I pondered the future. We were on the cusp of the year 2098, and everything was terrible. Police were sparse dots amongst the writhing throng of humanity. The ones you could get to respond to a call were often corrupt—looking to shake someone down or rape the remaining scraps of a scene. Allen would likely vie for a role in my operation—but that was something I feared.

While my service to humanity could be deemed a 'necessary evil', I wanted Allen to have no part in it. He was good. Too good to be torturing people and fucking severed heads. If I failed at everything else—and I likely *would*—I would not fail him. He deserved a chance at coming out the other end of this thing not being a total psychopath.

I strolled to my walk-in closet, my thick root swaying. My wardrobe was a sea of black suits and crimson ties. I slowly got dressed, buttoning up my slacks and dress shirt as I stared off into the distance. Dinner. What *were* we having for dinner, anyway? I hadn't eaten in two days, and the notion of sustenance had crumbled away in the nuclear fallout of my grief.

Whatever it was, it smelled delicious. Hunger reintroduced itself to my system, my stomach beginning to rumble and roil in weak protest. I absentmindedly finished up dressing and made my way downstairs. Just as I seated myself at the head of the mahogany dining table, Asimov strode into the room.

"Good evening, Master Leon. Today's feast is—" he said, pausing for—what was it? Dramatic effect?

"Ta-da!" Allen shouted cheerily, popping from around the corner with a tray in his hands. I was immediately impressed. This young man had perfectly recreated Asimov's Lasagna recipe. Steam billowed from the pillowy heaven atop the serving tray, a mountain of gooey cheese, savory bolognese sauce, and tender noodles. "That looks—*amazing*, kid. Very good job," I said with a proud grin.

Allen's face turned a shade more pink, and he fidgeted with his hands. "Oh, uh—thank you. Asy did most of the wor—"

"Oh, I most certainly did *not*," Asimov snapped, interrupting him mid-sentence. "Sir, I would be remiss if I didn't give this young man the credit that's due. He made this meal entirely on his own, down to the noodles." I grinned wider, my eyes going back to the boy. "That true, Allen?"

He slowly nodded, bashful under the spotlight of praise Asy and I had turned on him. "Well, I'm extremely proud of you. Let's dig in, kid. It looks and smells delicious," I said with my best-selling grin. He smiled, taking his seat and scanning the room anxiously. I let our android friend set the table and plate our portions.

As the fork was making its trajectory to my mouth, I noticed Allen watching on anxiously out the corner of his eye. I chewed on the healthy bite of cheesy goodness, letting out a contented groan. It was organic, but I *may* have hammed it up a bit to get him feeling comfortable. Every element was perfect—the meat was tender and well seasoned, the noodles a perfect al dente, the sauce and cheese ratio sublime.

"It's perfect, kid. Asy may get days off with you around."

"I'd hope not, sir," Asimov said with a pinch of sass. I laughed, patting the tabletop heartily. "Don't worry, I'd never let you gather dust." My android friend would have looked quite put out if he had expressions at that moment. Never joke about obsolescence to artificial intelligence. It makes them testy.

"*Gather. Dust?* Sir, I'd deactivate myself if ever I thought *that* would be the case! Wh-*" "Calm down, tin-head. I'm messing with you," I said through a mouthful of lasagna, a laugh bubbling up in my guts. He relented, nodding before taking his place near the kitchen doorway, in case either of us needed something. I took another steaming bite, savoring the delicious combinations of herbs, spices, and (most importantly) beef fat, which gave the entire dish a layer of richness that was immaculate.

"So, Allen—if this cooking thing is something you're interested in—I can arrange for you to go to a culinary institute when you're older," I said casually between bites. His eyes were saucers boring into my soul when I glanced up from my plate. "You don't want me to help *you?*" he asked with hurt in his voice. I shook my head, seeking to clarify things for him.

"Listen, kid—you can do anything you'd like to do. If that's cracking criminal skulls, great. But if not—there are many options for a talented young man that won't leave you broken or worse. You're not 'out of a job', so relax, okay?" He did, if a bit begrudgingly, his shoulders losing their tense position as he processed what I was telling him.

"I—I guess it'd be cool to learn how to cook more things. But I want to train with you. I want to save other kids like me," Allen said fiercely. I could feel his determination from across the table. His dark hair covered his eyes as he leaned forward and made his stance well known.

"I know I'm still weak, but I think I'm ready for *some* training, Leon. I don't want to wait. Waiting is just going to make it harder." I'll admit, I was impressed with him. He was articulate and driven. Some of those traits were undeniably charismatic, and why he was there. They were qualities required of someone doing the work that lay ahead of him.

"You're not weak, Al. Not in the slightest. It's only been three days, and already I can see you packing some weight on. That's good. I'll make you a deal. You listening?" I asked calmly. He nodded, his dark eyes patiently looking into mine.

"Give me a week. I have to go out of state for an operation. You weighed in at seventy-two pounds the day you arrived. Asy keeps charts. If you can hit an even eighty by the time I return, we'll begin your physical regime. A month of that, and I'll gauge whether or not you're ready for firearm training. How's that sound?"

I could see the boy trying not to explode out of his skin from excitement. Love bloomed in my chest with each passing moment in his presence. I'd give anything to feel those strong and pure emotions again. I supposed to myself that maybe I was trying to feel them vicariously through Allen. Whatever my angle, it felt good to see someone still *alive* inside.

"Yes, Leon! I'll eat good every day! Even the vegetables!" he shouted eagerly. I couldn't help but laugh at this. Al joined in, and then we both dug in to our dinner properly. If I survived my siege on Unit 403-7, we would enter a new era for vigilante justice. Hell would pay.

IV: ATL

After sending Allen to bed, I made my way to the office on the first floor. The stench of vomit was gone, thanks to Asimov's tireless cleaning, but the air was heavy in that room. Visions of me in a hallway slaughtering children stabbed my mind as I stood, petrified. With a great degree of restraint, I pushed those dark scenes away.

Unit 403-7 in Atlanta, Georgia—I entered the information into a GPS program on my computer, and awaited the results. Within twenty seconds, I had access to camera feeds, crime reports, and population statistics. It didn't take but a cursory glance to see that Atlanta was a shithole just as much as any other place. Unsurprisingly, it ranked number three in all the United States for human trafficking.

It was so easy to lose sight of the picture before. After what I uncovered on Vince's hard-drive, the roof was blown off of all my ill-conceived notions. The scale of Precious Cargo Productions was—colossal. Gargantuan. I'd never seen such a large web with so many vile people inhabiting it. As much as it pained me to admit, torture was going to have to take a backseat.

Logistically, it wouldn't get me anywhere to spend an hour per pedophile inflicting pain. Cliche though it may be, I was going to have to kill 'em all and let God sort 'em out. Minus the God part, I suppose. He never listened to me, anyway. I continued scanning all the information displayed, making mental notes of any landmarks or odd cases that could give me additional insights. Within two hours, I had everything I needed.

* * *

At 0700 hours, I entered the hangar at the back end of my property. For any casual flyovers, it looked like a high-end barn. Inside was a different story, altogether. Multiple Spiritwings sat neatly lined and ready to fly on the concrete slab. Above, the roof would open mechanically for takeoff. Tack that onto the suite of stealth software integrated into the hangar's central brain, and it was an extremely efficient and covert affair to take flight.

I walked over to the central hub, an array of supercomputers interlinked to provide top-tier technological support, guidance, and information relay. I input the flight coordinates, pressed 'execute', then walked to Spiritwing C. Looking upon the heavenly raptor, I felt a surge of pride and anticipation. It was a model for flying under the guise of 'Leon Crimson', but had all the toys I'd need under its banal appearance. After that week, nothing would remain the same.

Spiritwings pilot door opened automatically as I walked up to it. I climbed in, letting the machine do all the work for me. The engine roared to life, rotors beginning their revolutions that picked up in speed at a rapid and constant rate. On the dash, a display panel showed my flight path as well as the estimated time taken. An hour and a half, not bad.

"See you on the other side, kid," I murmured softly to myself as I glanced toward Crimson Manor. With that strange moment of—*humanity*—over, I engaged the flight-stick, letting the helicopter ascend. The roof's halves separated on mechanical arms, leaving a celestial port for my journey. I lifted from the hangar and accelerated away into the gloom.

* * *

Up high, the putridity of the world was eclipsed by the majesty of our reckoning at hand. Overpopulation and wasteful manufacturing had left very few trees that could be described as 'lush' or 'verdant'. The soil had blackened far below, hardened, acidic, hostile to any seed that dared attempt to take root. Whether I accomplished everything I wanted to, humanity was a short drop from its finale, regardless.

I flew on, taking in the small groves of trees that remained. *This* was the government's idea of conservation. It wasn't a joke, but if it had been, they would kill it during stand-up hour. *Let it all burn, as long as Allen lives to be an old man first,* I thought. Spiritwing C roared and sliced through the skyline like a razorblade opening a tender wrist.

* * *

"Right on time," I murmured to myself as the expansive sprawl of buildings came into view. Atlanta was once beautiful (if a bit overcrowded and rowdy at times), but *now*—now it was in utter ruins. Towers with chunks of outer wall missing lined the metropolis like rotting teeth in the mouth of a homeless street-fighter. Fires dotted the dark mass of clustered humanity, a few blue dots intermixed, giving the illusion of a law enforcement presence.

Unit 403-7 was on Northside, but in a city like that, there was *no* 'good' side of town. It was all gangs, pimps, prostitutes and the rare decent person just struggling to stay afloat in the sea of evil. I had reserved a penthouse suite about ten blocks away from my target. Five minutes of easy flying led me to the helipad atop Varaga Inn, where I touched Spiritwing down easily. I killed the engine, entering the security code for full lockdown before stepping out onto the roof. Gunfire and wails of inhuman anguish greeted my ears from the top of the tower.

No matter how hard I worked here, it'd never be a better place. I walked towards the roof entrance, pondering the purpose of life. If humanity only worsened with numbers, perhaps society was a faulty band-aid to give us the false hopes that we weren't all really animals beneath the layers. All those layers—wealth, achievement, doing the 'right' thing—they were window dressing for a house in flames.

"Good afternoon, Mr. Crimson," a man in a maroon suit said jovially to me as I entered the roof access doorway. His manner was mild, his ginger hair short-shaved and face well-groomed. His name was "Liam," according to the nametag pinned to the breast pocket of his coat. He smiled patiently, letting me get my bearings without expecting a prompt response.

"Good afternoon—Liam. Thanks for meeting me up here."

"Most certainly, sir. That's why they pay me the big bucks! Ha!," he said, putting on his best show-laugh. Already, I fucking despised him. *You can just throw him off the roof. Who would notice?* My eyes sharpened, and I did my best to shut out the Daemon's cruelly seductive suggestions.

"Well, I appreciate it, either way. I'm just one floor down, correct?" I asked, keeping my voice even. For anyone outside of my situation, all appearances had to be respected. I was just a businessman out on a bender for poker games and premium pussy. Why *else* would a multi-millionaire be in ATL?

"That is right, sir! Suite forty. The door is near the elevator, which should make it quite convenient to come and go with little hassle," Liam said proudly, as though *he* built and planned the fucking thing. A company man, truly tragic. The day people realize that it's all a work would be the moment that the puppetmaster's strings were finally severed. "Well, thanks, Liam. I'll be getting dressed and resting, then," I said as we walked to the elevator, pressing the 'down' button.

Muzak, beige and terrible, played over the speakers in the elevator. Liam stared forward like a well-trained dog as we descended to floor forty. I felt my limbs tingling, my heart racing. All of this was so very new to me. Never had I worked in a different city, altogether. The stench of Liam's cheap cologne was making me antsy to leave the confined space, and just as I felt a violent impulse re-surge, the bell dinged, and I was at my floor.

"Here you are, sir! If there's *anything* you need, ask for 'Liam' at the front desk," the ginger said in his best customer service voice, his smile wide, but his eyes lacking any light behind them. "Will do," I said, and as I stepped out of the elevator, he gently tugged at the sleeve of my coat. I turned, seeing a more

22

meaningful expression on his face, like he had a dirty secret he was dying to share.

"I mean anything, sir. No judgements are cast here at the Varaga Inn. Don't hesitate to call." I nodded, and as the doors closed, the smile on his face left a sinking feeling in the pit of my stomach. *Anything. In that tone, you know as well as I, Leon, that these cunts are in PCP. Don't deny it.*

I couldn't, no matter how much I'd have liked to. Now was not the time, however. Unit 403-7 was top priority, everything else was but a distraction. I walked to my room, which, as described, was very close in proximity to the elevators.

It was as opulent a room as expected, given a man of my means and station. Plush jade carpet covered the floors, the gilded wallpaper screaming 'decadence'. The scent of pot-pourri floated throughout the massive suite. I spat on the floor, setting my bag on the bed. After a moment, I decided to live the 'normal' life in Atlanta for a while. Darkness would be my ally as I infiltrated the den of evil.

* * *

I spent the following hours drinking bourbon at the hotel bar, then having a filet mignon as the time drew near. Being drunk didn't concern me. After my last excursion, I'd introduced a drug that would keep me at full operational capacity for hours, maybe days if needed.

The trip back to my suite was uneventful, a sea of falsely cheerful faces on display with no hint of shame or self aware-ness. All of these lives hung precariously from a cliff, yet there they were—posturing and smiling. *It'd be so much better if everyone was fucking dead.* At the Daemon's remark, I was indifferent. He wasn't wrong, but I had to keep driving on hoping something good could come from this hellish world.

Everything in the Varaga was exhaustingly gilded and grandiose for the sake of spectacle. I kept my eyes trained on the floor, entering the elevator. The door had almost closed, when a pair of drunk cunts stumbled in. I concealed a grimace at the stench of the alcohol emanating from them as they sucked face with all the skill and grace of a ballet dancer with cerebral palsy.

The man was an upper class Caucasian, balding, average build. His partner was clearly an escort. She was far too beautiful for him, black, with gracious curves and wavy hair that flowed to her midriff. A silky lavender nightdress clung to her ample assets, her makeup disheveled from the gratuitous display.

"You gonna suck this fat, white cock?" he breathed loudly to her, either oblivious or indifferent to my presence. She gave a false moan of 'approval', shoving a hand down the front of his pants and massaging his prick with the overly enthusiastic motions of a tried-and-true vet. I stared forward, hoping they'd get off soon, but knowing it was likely they were in for the long haul, just like me.

"You got that video, right?" he asked a bit more quietly, though it was loud enough for me to hear and get my hackles raised in apprehension. "Yeah. Costs—a bit," she said, eyeing me as though suddenly alerted to my presence. The drunk douchebag waved indifferently in my direction, saying, "This fucking guy is richer than I am, don't worry about it. Right, bud?"

I eyed him slowly, feeling bile wash the back of my throat

at his amiable nature, his presumed comradery. Even if every rich fuck *was* buddy-buddy, I never considered myself a part of that society. Especially given how many of the cunts were apparently connected to Precious Cargo Productions. Now, everyone other than myself was a target, and a potential threat to all I stand for.

"Sure, I wasn't even paying attention," I lied calmly. The pair of writhing mouth-breathers giggled, going back to their ham-fisted foreplay. We were near floor forty then, my hellish exposure coming to a grateful end. "PCP-made, right?" he asked in hushed tones. "Mhm," she said, jerking his cock smoothly, her stroke only moving visibly about three inches or so.

They're everywhere, Leon. Everywhere. Are you going to look past this one, too? Hmm? Should we just say 'let bygones be bygones' and give the pedophiles a break this once?

Over my dead fucking body, I thought. The elevator dinged. We had reached floor forty.

V: Splish Splash, I Was Taking A Bath

I let him take reign then, those three little letters sending me into a berserk. "PCP, good shit," he said through my numb lips. The pair of twats chuckled giddily like we were all in on a naughty secret, their pupils expanding in a debased form of lust reserved for those of the ninth circle of Hell. "I've got a nice suite. Why don't we—do some blow and get some blowing done?" I asked, my seductive smirk working its magic on those soft-brained neanderthal cunts.

"Listen, my guy—that sounds fun, but she's top-shelf, and—" he began, before the escort swept her smokey eyes to mine. "Baby, for a rail and a good dick, it'll be no extra charge." she said through glossy lips, her chest heaving in lust-filled excitement. The john smiled dumbly, shrugging. "I guess that's that, then. Let's go to your suite."

I nodded casually, leading the way to my room. I slid the keycard, trying the knob once the reader beeped softly. We entered, the couple of soon-to-be tragic *lovers* trailing behind, giggling and speaking softly. Casually, I pointed to the massive bathtub, the walls behind it mirrored. "Make yourselves comfortable. I'll get the blow," I said, heading to the walk-in closet where I had stashed my travel bag.

They wasted no time, stripping as the man got the water running. Giggles drifted to me, and the sound of her throating his cock greedily. He moaned softly, and I pushed my need to kill down deep. Patience is a virtue when you've got multiple lives at stake. I lined up a half-dozen thick lines of Columbian pure on a small circular mirror, strolling back out with a jaunty grin. I hoped it was convincing, if only to get what I needed from this.

"Lines?" I asked in caked-on charm as I lowered the snorting tray for them to inspect. "Don't mind if I do," the escort said after letting his half-hard prick slip from her sumptuous mouth. She snorted the coke back proficiently, pinching her nostrils as she sucked the drip back and panted in pleasure. "If you can't beat 'em, join 'em!" the small-dicked loser said with a shit-eating grin.

I took my line to keep up the charade, letting their comfort slip in and make them complacent. I had to be cautious, move slowly. One slip-up, and they'd bolt like gazelle scattering at a lioness's approach. It was working. The duo slipped into the tub, and she began jerking him off as he leaned his head back against the wall, sighing contentedly.

Shit or get off the pot. No time like the present.

"Mind if I put that vid on?" I asked casually, pulling my coat off and loosening my tie. The man looked indifferent, eyeing his masturbator curiously. She looked at me, her eyes analyzing me, sizing me up. "One million dollar wire transfer, and I'll get it out," she said flatly.

27

"We splitting this fifty-fifty, or—?" he asked bluntly. I hid my annoyance beneath the surface. What was half a million dollars for peace of mind? "Sure, but no funny business," I said, directing the latter half sternly to the dark goddess stroking a milk-toast penis beneath a thin film of bubbles.

"Scout's honor," she said in bemusement, her arm continuing to move its well-rehearsed motion. I stood there, pretending to stress over a financial decision for what I deemed to be a socially appropriate amount of time among such degenerates. "You've got a deal," I said, pulling my wire-fob from my wallet. They both stared upon my rippling muscles, drooling at the scars and snow-white skin.

"Oh, this is gonna be fuckin' *hot*," the man said, leaning forward abruptly to fish through his pants pocket outside the tub. The escort stopped jerking him off long enough to produce a fob-scanner from her clutch. Within a minute, the two of us were half a million dollars poorer. "Cool," the dark seductress said upon verifying the transfer. "Put it on and get back to sucking this dick!" the chrome dome exclaimed.

He was truly pathetic, with all the enthusiasm of an over-eager highschool senior about to cum his pants on prom night. Sudsy bubbles slalomed down the escort's ample, jiggling ass as she produced a jump drive from her clutch and inserted it into the television. The tv powered on, a mellow jingle playing that belied the violent precipice we were nearing. "This is heavy shit," she said, eyeing the both of us with warning.

"We're big boys, I think we can handle it," fuckface chuckled. I nodded, feeling my pulse raise as the world around me was escalating into fight-or-flight. She pressed a button, and the jump drive began playing the video that would decide their fates. As always, it started with an establishing shot. A little girl was bound in rope, her backside exposed in the frame.

Cold, stabbing waves of dread seeped into my coursing blood. Whatever happened next, I was certain that I was going to come out the other end of this thing more fucked up. It was inevitable. No one makes it through without scars, and I've made many return trips. "What's your name?" a scum-laden voice asked the helpless child.

"L-Leah," she whimpered.

* * *

I couldn't tell you how long I was frozen. However long it was, the 'now' came roaring up to me in a rush of blood and a magmatic burst of hatred. I turned to go back into the closet, doing everything in my power not to hear sweet Leah being abused for the pleasure of monsters. Digging through the go-bag, I found the perfect tool to get shit started right. Today was my re-dedication to serve the Daemon in full earnest.

Just on the other side, I could hear the man moaning as the whore sucked his cock. They were just grooving along to child pornography. *For a predator, pretense only matters if they're luring prey. Like you, my little Leon.* I shook his venom away, ensuring the weapon was ready. Do or die.

Like a lightning bolt from the blue, I burst purposefully out of the closet, aiming my weapon at the writhing worms. "Look at me, and listen *really* fucking closely," I snarled. Their eyes were upon me, the time for fellatio and pedophilia now at an end. "The child on that fucking video was—a friend. And I'm irritable, besides, so—tell me everything you know on Precious Cargo Productions, and you'll get *this*," I said, raising the sawed-

29

off shotgun, "instead of taken apart with blades. Sound good?"

"I just receive dead drops for the jump drives," the prostitute began, her body trembling in fear. "Go on." "Well, I know that they have a Unit close to here where they handle all the tech shit. My job is just distribution. I don't have direct access to that money. I just receive—"

"A cut?" I asked, keeping my voice flat. "Y-yeah." "Okay, thanks for that," I said, pushing the barrels against her forehead and pulling the trigger before she could react. The boom was deafening, her skull reduced to mush by two barrels loaded with razor-shrapnel shells. Blood painted the mirror behind the tub. The man was silent, frozen as I stared at myself in the mirror, bathed in blood and desperately yearning for more. So much more.

"Okay, so we know what *she* had to say," I said with a smirk. He trembled, hyperventilating and doing his best to avoid eye contact with me. Blood gushed in an arc from the hooker's stump of a neck, her body stuck mid-pose. Brain flecks were in every conceivable nook and cranny of the tub. "What do *you* have to say there—*buddy*?" He began stammering, and I strode to the closet, picking up my trusty tanto and flicking the sheath off in one fluid motion.

"Man, I just—the fucking *bitch*," he spluttered, pointing at our dearly departed, "said that she had some premium cp stock. I was just trying to fuck a black bitch! I didn't—" I had heard enough. With a mighty downward arc, I severed his right arm with the short blade. Blood geysered from his torso as he wailed. My next swipe severed his head, which splashed into the water, floating. The dumb-founded terror I instilled was his last expression. *As it should be. Good work, Leon. You're a loyal servant.*

VI: Unit 403-7

I stripped my clothing, tossing it into the blood-filled tub. My choices were limited in terms of corpse removal, given Atlanta was not my city. Liam said Varaga didn't judge, so maybe that was a choice. And if he was in with Precious Cargo Productions as well—I'd gladly add another cadaver to the stack. It wouldn't be the first time I've had to manhandle the help.

I took a whore-bath, wiping myself clean before changing into my combat rig. The mask could wait until I was clear of any hallway cameras when I moved. The Daemon had gone silent after the slaughter, and no one called or said 'boo' about the fucking shotgun blast. What a time to be rich and powerful. I grabbed my laptop from the bag in the closet, doing more research as I waited for night to fall.

* * *

31

It was time. I moved silently from my suite to the stairwell at the end of the east wing. By the time I reached the first floor, I was feeling like hammered dogshit. No more benders or wasting time, I told myself. It was embarrassing. What kind of 'hero' gets winded on stairs?

I reached the fire exit door, pulling the retractable cable from my belt and bypassing the alarm. Silently, I left Varaga Inn, walking into the darkened expanse of a brand new Hell. Once I was well and clear of Varaga, my true face came out, completing me. Two blocks, and I'd be in range to observe and cripple an integral organ of the beast which I sought to slay.

Into the shadows I went, hugging my silhouette to the edges of darkened alleyways. In every direction, I could hear shouting, gunfire, sex, rape. The sewers were clogged, water pooling on the street surface. If people still used conventional land vehicles, *that* would be a major issue. Any time I caught motion, I would shrink against whatever building I was walking beside.

Two blocks took thirty minutes to traverse in this way, but it was necessary. On my person, I had bugs for gathering hard data, a bypass box for obtaining and infiltrating their IP address. Just in case, I had a Kriss Vector chambered in .45 ACP slung on my back, with six backup magazines. All told, I had two hundred and ten rounds. I hoped it didn't need to use them just yet, skulking to the intersection.

I peeked around the corner, and Unit 403-7 was finally in my sights. Unlike many of the crumbling, destitute structures around it, the unit was intact. Hell, it was in *good* shape—a sign of organization and undoubted manpower that I mentally noted. I expected nothing less of a center for an organization conducting such sensitive operations.

Scanning the entrance, I saw four armed guards. They all wore gray fatigues, with AK-47's and bandoleers loaded down with .762 magazines. I pulled one bug from a cargo pocket, activating it with a button press. The metal sphere rolled of its own accord, heading towards the building. I ducked back behind the corner for cover and waited.

In less than thirty seconds, at least two of the gunmen opened fire on the bug. These cunts were good, and very well equipped if they noticed it that quickly. I listened intently for any chatter and heard none. Tight-lipped. They were clearly military trained. I had my work cut out for me.

That ruled out any notion of a grandiose 'go in, guns blazing' strategy instantly. Luckily, I had a million little ways to get around a door guarded by crack-shots. I glanced at my watch, noting a side entry on my map. Silently, I made my way up to another building, skirting around Unit 403-7's side the long way. Five minutes of sneaking, and I was there.

The door before me wasn't guarded, but that's because it didn't have to be. A security panel was set into the wall—top-notch stuff, make no mistake. I sent out an electro-magnetic pulse from my watch, finding a signature for a surveillance camera. This would be the way in, as long as I set the proper groundwork.

I pilfered through my pockets, finding the bypass and powering it on. It resembled a metallic hockey puck, with a few discreet buttons. Within a few minutes, I had deactivated the camera, severing its visibility from the master control grid. Relieved it hadn't taken longer, I skulked to the lock, scanning around for any sound or movement.

The alleyway was quiet, dark, and lacking any massive mounds of debris or rubble that was plentiful everywhere else

I had been. I connected the retractable cable from my belt to the control panel, manually slicing the lock function through an interface on my watch. A hollow click sounded out, and I tried the door. It opened up right away.

I pulsed again, relaying a mirror feed of an empty hallway into the security system. It wouldn't stop anyone from knowing something was up in person, but it would keep PCP from knowing who hit them until it was too late. I walked with purpose, mindful of the volume of my footsteps. Every few feet, I would halt and listen for any through traffic.

As I had hoped, Unit 403-7 conducted all its encryption and distribution operations during daytime hours. Anyone I found while running surveillance would be part of a skeleton crew. It didn't take a genius to know why they'd bother keeping a night crew at all—protecting their database. If a leak came from that place, it'd be global news— corrupt governments, or not.

The corridors were a bizarro parallel to those of 378-6—where there was once trash and shattered bottles now was gray pristine carpet. Doors for undersized apartments were now replaced by doors for massive office chunks. I scanned the room plate numbers, taking mental notes of anything that could be crucial. So far it was banal horseshit, the kind of thing most people wouldn't expect a global organization for pedophiles to implement.

Human Resources, Supply Acquisitions, Accounting, and so on—everything a growing company needs to keep on functioning. I reached the edge of the corridor, slinging the Kriss Vector into my hands and switching the selector to 'fire'. After a count to four, I peaked quickly around the corner. In relief, I walked out in the clear. There was no one around so far, and it only added to my mounting tension and dread.

I popped the control panel next to the elevator, implementing a bypass that showed room functions, names, numbers. Many of the areas in the building were simply named 'storage', which could only mean one thing—server farms and heaps of interlink hard-drives full of child pornography, snuff, and mixtures of the two. When 'command center' came across the list of room names, I stopped. That would be where the bugs would do their best work.

According to my display, it was on the twentieth floor. I stepped into the elevator, pressing the 'up' button with a death-grip on my submachine gun. The ascent was glacial, hatefully slow. Muzak again greeted me—bland, soulless—everything on brand for PCP. I chambered a round, the metallic *CHUNK* giving me a moment of inner peace.

When the elevator dinged, I hugged the right wall, listening as the doors slid open for anyone nearby. I heard something, but it wasn't close enough to cause panic just yet. My watch was earning its keep yet again, giving me two heat signatures for the floor. I stepped out, Kriss Vector at high-ready.

Every area looked the same—stainless steel doors, dull gray carpet, and runners of cables, neatly sheathed and running along the ceiling joint of every wall. If I was a gambling man—and in the line of work I do, I'm most certainly *not*—I wagered that over half of the video distribution and funds transfers took place in the building I was scouting. "Man, do they *really* need to keep six of us for night shift? We have guys guarding the door, and everything's so fucking encrypted a *genius* would be hard-pressed to crack our systems," a whiney voice said ahead on my right.

I paused, crouching with my weapon raised, assessing where he was, exactly. It was a break room. Of course. I noticed then that the room I needed to access was directly across from it. "Are you *really* bitching about easy money?" a huskier, meaner voice responded. "Well, I wouldn't say that I'm *bitching*—" came the prissy retort before being cut off abruptly.

"Of fucking course, *you* wouldn't, Neville. You're too much of a pussy to even call yourself one, and that's one of your *main* problems. You're one of those little bitches who thinks he's not a bitch. Drink your coffee, jerk off to whatever sick shit you have on that laptop, and leave me the fuck alone so I can sleep." A pause laden with social tension drifted to me. I smirked, pondering how men in such a line of work could be so weak and—*ordinary*. "Fine, I'll do that. Night, Steve." I heard the 'Neville' fellow stand up, and promptly hid behind a large trash can, my weapon tight against my chest.

The God I often speak of (but seldom believe in) gave me a break. Neville walked past, head buried in his laptop as he walked away. My breathing was tight, my anxiety high. Once I knew the coast was truly clear(I could tell by the security chief's loud snoring in the breakroom), I walked to Room 2099 and let myself in. I had arrived at the nerve center for the world's largest child pornography ring.

At the command center, I quickly got to work—I powered on the remaining bugs I had stashed in my pocket. They rolled off in separate directions, embedding themselves discreetly into wire clusters. With them in play, I could compile and harvest data from the comfort of my room. It took all of five minutes, and I had the building's primary IP address and my bugs fully integrated into the computer systems. I sent out another pulse once finished with my work, seeing only two blips—one for Steve, one for Neville.

With as much caution as I could muster, I crept back to the

elevator. It seemed to take longer to open than any elevator I'd dealt with prior or since. When the bell dinged, I jumped despite myself. Something along the way had left me a much jumpier operator. I had to rectify that. I needed my fire rekindled, and it felt like the world around me was stomping it out.

Once I reached the ground floor, I hastily made my way to the door I had come in through. The noise of a city at war greeted me as I slunk back into the shadows whence I came. Thirty minutes later, and I was back in my suite. "I forgot I had guests," I chuckled softly to myself. I stared at the hacked up cadavers having a sensual soak, pondering what the rest of my night had in store.

VII: Cabin Fever

You've been needing to use that gorgeous cock, Leon. All that pent up cum needs to be pumped into a weeping hole. Don't you want to wear someone like a pinkie ring and leave them breathless? Don't you want to cause pleasure in equal parts to the pain you dole out?

I stood, listening begrudgingly to the Daemon, who had deemed four in the morning an opportune time to give me commands. Whatever He wanted, it would have to wait. I needed sleep desperately, which meant I needed morphine to overpower the residual cocaine and adrenaline jolting my mind. Getting in and out of a secure location wasn't anything *new*, but it always left me riding an incredible high.

I walked by the bath-time blood orgy to the closet, grabbing my pill tray from the go-bag stored there. I kicked my boots across the room, stripping the fatigues off. Once I was down to my boxers, I half-heartedly dove into the king-sized bed and popped two twenty milligram Morphine tablets. Though it tasted fucking horrendous, I crushed the pills between my back molars to make them kick in more quickly.

You're really going to deny everything that makes you who you are? Where's Mr. HardAss? What have you done with the man who gladly fucked a man's face after unhinging his jaw and filing his teeth away?

"Go away, please. I'm so tired. I've given you so much. Can't that just be *enough* for now?"

Silence bloomed, enclosing my nerve endings in the icy chill of existential dread. I was awaiting a reply from what was essentially *myself*. This was a can of worms I was nowhere near ready to unpack. No amount of medication in the world could cure the warring hemispheres of my mind as they raced towards a nuclear head-on collision. Who would win—the empath, lover, romantic? Or—the sadist, backstabber, ruthless cutthroat?

The part of myself that I hoped was the *real* me hoped good was enough for a person to get through life. That person was who got held down and raped like a Nazi in a prison shower. The other—the other made me the efficient killer and avenger I was. 'Duality of Man' always seemed like a load of pseudo-philosophical tripe to me when I was younger. Growing older, my chains to the other side of the veil were ever-shortening—and it all began making more sense.

I was at an impasse—I could let the Daemon hold total control, say "Damn the consequences", or—change fundamental blocks of who I was. Allen deserved a guardian who didn't have intrusive thoughts about hurting him. He deserved the world, and who I was in that crucial moment simply couldn't give it to him. Not yet.

Something was odd about the Daemon's musings, however. There wasn't a lick of violent insinuation or malevolent undertones. The unfortunate thing about psychosis is that your command voices don't come and go at your convenience. As a rule of thumb, I'd say they only come when it's at the *worst* possible time. So—I lay in the cool dark of the suite—awaiting sleep or His return, whichever came first. The Sand Man took his toll, and slumber brought me into its hungry embrace.

* * *

I awoke around noon, the smell of blood and scented bubble bath stale and beginning to become oppressive. I yawned, stretching out my stiff arms, working my taut back. For an exclusive suite, they used terrible mattresses. I always slept best at home, the lumpy pillow another reminder of what I was missing out on. I stared ponderously at the corpses for a moment, then called the front desk with the bedside phone.

My call rang a grand one and a half times before a nauseatingly cheery voice greeted me on the other end. "Varaga Inn, Liam speaking. How may we help you today, Mr. Crimson?" "Just the man I wanted to speak to. I need assistance. It'd be best if you came up and we discussed it in person," I said. Liam immediately said that it was no problem at all, and that I'd see him within the next fifteen minutes.

"Well, Liam—you're either a cunt or an evil cunt. Ball's in your court," I said to myself, getting out of bed. I grabbed my fatigues and mask, storing them in the go-bag underneath a few changes of clean civilian attire. I glanced in the mirror over the sink, and decided what I saw was good enough. Why bother churching any of this up? I was calling for in-house body disposal, after all.

Within ten minutes, a light rapping came at my suite door.

"Fucker's quick," I mumbled softly before opening the door. Liam stood there, cheesing like he'd won a sweepstakes trip to Hawaii (before it was hit with a nuclear strike from orbit). "You rang?" he asked, his fake smile sliding wider. "Yeah, but it's—sensitive. You *sure* this is a 'come-as-you-are'-type establishment?" I asked, feigning fear as I gazed upon the flattened visage of a wolf in sheep's clothing.

"Oh, don't worry about *that*," he said, gently worming his way into the suite. When he looked at the blood-soaked tub, all he did was let out a low whistle and pause to think. I stood there, analyzing any tells he might be giving. The man was emotionless behind his customer service mask—a great white shark in the darkened depths of the sea.

"Is this going too far?" I asked, affecting a tremble in my voice. I had to sell this thing. "Oh, Mr. Leon, this is *nothing*," Liam said with a hollow grin. Without hesitation, he pulled his phone from his pocket and made a call. Three minutes and a few code words later, he hung up the phone with a cheeky smile. "These," he said, pointing to the dead whore and john, "will be gone in the next two hours. All you have to do is transfer $100,000 and stay out of the room until, say—four p.m. Sound good, sir?"

Greedy little ginger minge, I thought to myself as I nodded, pretending to fumble for my transfer fob. I paid him his fee, grabbing my bag from the closet. The transfer took all of five minutes. After that, I headed out into Atlanta to kill some time.

The joyous sounds of plastic people going about their lives was a cacophony on aching ears. I made myself small, keeping my eyes on my surroundings as I headed to the restaurant on the first floor. All the perfumes and colognes in the air overwhelmed my senses. Behind every smile was another lie yet to be revealed.

I ordered an entrée of chicken parmigiana, tipping the beady-eyed waiter as he set the food down and telling him I'd like to be left alone. He graciously obliged, slinking back into the kitchen with an oafish grin upon his acne-marred face. In terms of presentation, the meal was beautiful—but my appetite was yo-yoing from all the substance abuse, adrenaline, and stress.

I went through the motions, cutting small pieces of chicken breast and eating it with fork-twirls of noodles. By the time I had finished, I only needed to kill another thirty minutes. If I stayed in that restaurant, I was going to go insane, so I strolled to the help desk and checked out the in-house entertainment. Much of it was the sort of thing I'd consider torture—stuffy jazz bands, bingo, speed-dating. Then my eyes fell upon the arcade listed, and I knew what I could do to kill some time.

Neon signs from over a century ago hung on every free inch of wall space in the arcade. Looking around, I felt a small wave of sadness at how empty it was. When I found the gaming pc section, I sat down, downloading everything I'd need to have a good time. Brutal Doom booted up, and I began mowing demons down with the speed of hatred. Their chunky pixelated sprites were gorgeous, the blood decals and gore effects of the mod sublime. For a while, I forgot who Leon was. All I wanted to do was rip and tear.

Many fools would dismiss the game purely on the merit of its age and graphics. They were morons. No other game in the first-person shooter genre even held a candle to the pure magic that Doom possessed, modded or not. Motion was fluid, the controls the perfect blend between tight and floaty. I blew skulls off in rapid succession, feeling my cock engorge and shift in my pants at all the beautiful gore on display. The MIDI score was a fiery onslaught of nineteenth century metal, and it fit the action on screen to a t.

By the time I had made it to Episode Three, I had killed another hour. With a quick glance at my watch, I was satisfied with the time. If the bodies and evidence weren't gone by the time I reached my room, I'd have been shocked. I made my way back up to floor forty, grateful that no drunk wastes of life barged in. I keyed my way into the suite, and it looked like a brand new place.

"Not bad," I mused aloud. I checked my belongings, finding no evidence of tampering or pilfering. Whoever Liam had called was an utter professional. I lay on the bed, staring at the roof. Sleep crept upon me, bringing with it images of demons and children being slaughtered with a clawhammer.

VIII: A Week In the Hole

I awoke the next day at five in the morning. The toll of my benders and late-night excursions had come crashing down upon me with a vengeance. My mouth was dry, my head pounding. I stayed in the same spot for well over six hours after, turning over the events of the past week in my mind. It was truly mind-boggling how many things could change in such a brief span of time.

Friendships could end in a roar of flames and shouting, homes could crumble from natural disaster. Worst of all— you could wake up realizing that maybe you weren't *that* much better than the prey you hunted. The latter had been wracking every fiber of my being, playing a sorrowful symphony on my languishing soul. If I didn't shake off the guilt soon, suicide would creep into the back of my mind. It often had before, and now—now the stakes were higher than they'd ever been before.

Around ten p.m, I pulled my laptop out of the bag and set it up on the ebony nightstand. A few keystrokes later, and I was inside Unit 403-7's systems, combing for intel. The sooner I got the master list of operations locations, the sooner I could sever the serpent's head. More importantly, the sooner I could switch the bugs over to 'detonate' mode. That was where the fun *truly* began. Running surveillance was bland work.

Hours ticked by as I listened to chunks of picked up audio. Much of it was bog-standard office chatter, which I skimmed before flagging as 'n/a' to streamline my data-mining. Most of the fucks spoke on the same thing everyone else did—football, the flavor of the month popstar that big media was pushing, or whether someone had caught the most recent episode of whatever shit people watched nowadays. I groaned in annoyance and boredom while leaving no stone unturned.

For three days, I had kept myself holed up in the suite. I had foregone manual data-scrubbing, letting the software do all the heavy lifting. Millions of strands of data processed a minute, and I still could not get but a taste of that which I sought.

I stared off into the void for a while, truly reveling in the gray nebula I floated amongst. The Daemon had stayed silent, for which I was also grateful. In a week and a half, I had killed over forty people. If *that* wasn't enough, then I was a complete lost cause. I love violence—what red-blooded American doesn't? There was a limit, however—it would be a cold day in Hell before I just started feeding anyone with a pulse into a wood chipper for amusement.

On the fourth day, something finally caught my interest in the millions of files clogging PCP's systems. It was a miracle they hadn't had a server meltdown, especially given the high volume of content they stored and transmitted. I began delving into a file hub titled 'Master Site List'. If not for my software, it'd have likely slipped through the cracks. "Here goes nothing," I said to the empty suite that smelled of whiskey and the musk of my neglect.

My stomach dropped as I scanned the lists. There were five *hundred* operations locations in PCP. A wave of nausea stabbed me relentlessly. I clutched my head, anxiety racking me for all I was worth. How in the *fuck* was one man supposed to take down something so—*gargantuan*? Despite all the progress I had made, I wept.

Why are you crying again, Leon? Did you expect anything less from a global organization? Are we re-growing the naivety that left you in the state you're in now? Ill-advised, I'd say.

"Please, just let me fucking FEEL!" my shout reverberated from the walls, splintering my despair and positioning it around me like a whirlwind of knives. The Daemon backed off some, thankfully. I let the tears flow, purging the pain from myself as I hid underneath the comforter for a spell. I fell asleep again, the visions of all my evils laid at my feet by a hellhound that wagged its tail happily.

* * *

Day six. Shit or get off the pot. I compiled all the locations and personnel listed per location into an encrypted file and transmitted it to Crimson Manor. Asy would undoubtedly have it organized in a tidy spreadsheet by the time I returned home. I'd activate the bug's secondary function once I was safely in the air. I had one more unaddressed issue to resolve before leaving Atlanta, however.

I picked up the bedside phone, calling the front desk. Again, the phone rang two times before being promptly answered. "Liam, front desk. How may I help you?" I let the Daemon take control, laying on the charm and concocting a quick and easily sellable lie. "Hey, Liam. I just read a diagnostic scan on my helicopter, and I may need someone to help me take off. Could you meet me topside, please?"

Liam paused, doing his customary processing ritual for about thirty seconds before responding. Whether or not he was involved in PCP, something was—*off* about him. Something was sinister, and that's coming from a serial killer who tortures people for snuff films. "Sure thing. Need a jumper box?" he asked, helpful as always.

"Yeah, thanks. I'll see you on the roof. Bye," I said, hanging up. I quickly packed any scattered belongings remaining into my go-bag. After one last look through for anything I might have missed, I dropped the key card on the stand near the door and walked out into the corridor. Liam had better answer my questions well, or I'd add another body to the hall of Hell I kept well-stocked.

* * *

The seasons were changing. Atop Varaga Inn, I could feel the plummeting temperatures, the wind icy blades slicing a chill into my bones. I stowed the bag onto Spiritwing C and awaited Liam's arrival. I felt conflicted—the naïve child hidden in the corridors of my soul wanted him to just be a sleazebag who's used to rich assholes offing people. The Daemon wanted him to be an employee of PCP. Either way, I would get to the bottom of things soon.

Liam walked out onto the rooftop, his plastic smile radiating falsity. "If it's the battery, I blame the temperature drop," he said off-handedly as he approached me. "Yeah, that's a good possibility," I said casually. Once he was in grabbing distance, I let my true plans come through. "So, Liam—you work for Precious Cargo Productions?"

His face went red, his eyes panicked. "Wh-why would you think that, sir?" he asked, his acting shit-tier. "Because a guy who can have two cadavers dealt with in less than four hours is a guy who's connected. What would be more profitable than being a part-time lackey for a black industry that makes trillions a year? Hmm?" I asked, letting the facade of 'Goodguy Leon' fall away. My eyes burned holes into his as I awaited his response.

"I-I am. But I have *nothing* to do with their product. I just outsource their crime scene department for sticky situations," Liam said, sweat pouring down his pale, doughy face. It was the first time I had seen the cunt react emotionally to, well, *anything*. His story was much like all the other cockroaches scurrying the slums of that vile city.

"If a bomber plane drops an A-bomb on a city, does the GPS system get a free pass?" I asked, savoring the micro-expressions he was shifting through. He didn't know it was already over for him. "No matter, Liam. You help make the car move, so you're part of the problem."

Without warning, I caught him in the jaw with a powerful right hook. He collapsed into a heap on the roof. I powered on Spiritwing C, letting the rotors spin up to speed. Liam's breathing was deep—he'd likely be out for hours after a punch like that. I had much different plans, however.

Grunting from the dead weight, I hoisted Liam overhead.

Once the blades of the helicopter were close enough, I lifted his head. The rotors shredded it into a pulp of tissue, blood, and bone in an instant. I was showered in the burst of primal flow, lowering his corpse to my shoulder and walking to the edge of the roof. "So long, ginger twat," I said halfheartedly before throwing his headless body off the roof. It plummeted to the depths below, where he'd likely embed into the concrete. It was time to head out.

IX: Homeward Bound

Spiritwing C lifted off the roof of Varaga Inn, and as I ascended, the woes of the city beneath me shrank to a scale of insignificance. Unit 403-7 loomed on the right, only thirty seconds of flight away. I pushed the chopper a quarter mile out, then set it to hover. On the dash, I input a sequence to activate the bugs.

The signal didn't take long to relay, and I watched the progress bar slowly fill on the screen in the dash. Then, there was a boom. It was earth shatteringly loud, gouts of flame pluming into the heavens. The building crumbled in upon itself, black smoke billowing and coating the entire city in an acrid layer of toxins and cinders.

Chunks of concrete crumbled to the depths of waterlogged streets below, like God's righteous meteors. Even from a distance, I could see how the tinted and tempered windows had shrapnel-blasted themselves. Those below were surely dead. *This is a numbers game. What's a few people to take out thousands of pedophiles?* "Nothing at all," I said to my Daemon.

I grinned, and felt my cock engorge, spreading down my leg. The warmth and adrenaline had me incredibly aroused. "One down, four hundred and ninety-nine to go," I said to myself. I engaged the helicopter, and flew towards home, where I had a boy's progress to check upon. As I flew, I took a moment to think about something that was *good* for a change—I had something to look forward to.

Trees in man-made control clusters zoomed by far below, concrete and tar sending ripples of dancing heat making the earth's curvature dance for Daddy. I scanned the radar for any nearby aircraft. The coast was clear. I accelerated, taking the route home.

* * *

Crimson Manor drew into view, and I slowed Spiritwing C and activated the roof hatch with a button press on the dash. It opened, and I let the helicopter gradually decline, lowering to the landing pad with a soft bump. I killed the engine, listening to the rotors' revolutions gradually decline and breathed a sigh of relief. Though I was never truly *happy*—whatever the fuck *that* means—it felt truly good to be home.

By the time I got inside, Asimov was standing by to greet me. "Excellent to see you, sir! I hope it was a success?" he asked, grabbing my bag politely and letting me lead the way. "It was, Asy, thanks. Their central tech center is neutralized. We have the master list for ops centers and key operatives for PCP. We've still got a long way to go, but—it feels like we have

51

a shot to really *change* something for once," I answered as we walked up the grand stairwell, pride rising in my chest.

"I'm proud to be part of your team, sir. It is truly an honor." He stood beside my bedroom door, awaiting dismissal with my go-bag in his hand. "I wouldn't be able to do this thing without you. I hope you know that. How's Allen?" I asked, beckoning him to follow as I walked into the bedroom. I began changing from my travel clothes as he updated me on the state of things since I had left.

"He has been eager to earn your approval for training, sir. As of seven a.m. this morning, he has hit a weight of eighty-three pounds." I let out an impressed whistle. "Kid really wants to do this," I said, pulling my robe on and stepping into my slippers. "That's really all I needed to see—and he surpassed my expectations. I guess I'll break the news to him."

"Oh, that is marvelous, sir! He's in the game room right now, sir. When he learned of your gaming collection, he lost it—" "Of course he did! He's a pubescent boy!" I said, chuckling. Asy imitated respectfully, matching my energy. "That's good, thank you. Will you tidy this, please?" "Of course, sir. What would you like for dinner?"

Now *that* was a good question. I turned it over in my mind, weighing the options. Luckily for me, there was a five star cooking team living under my roof. Anything was on the table. I felt that something simple and robust would do the trick. The following day was going to be physically grueling for Allen and myself.

"I think I'm going to have to go with spaghetti bolognese and some cheesy garlic bread, my man. With all the cardio we'll be doing tomorrow, those carbohydrates will be crucial." "Absolutely, Master. I shall see that it is my best one yet!"

Asimov gathered my dirty clothes, taking them to the washroom after bowing to me. It felt—*good* to be home. For the first time in—probably *decades*. I walked back down the grand stairwell, letting my eyes devour the comforting sights of a place custom-tailored to comfort *me*. The wooden railing was polished, smoother than stone under my hand. It was cool to the touch, and the scent of Nag Champa incense pulled me into its embrace.

The games room was on the west wing of Crimson Manor, a side I seldom visited anymore. To be transparent, I wasn't sure *why*. I just had—bad feelings about that side of the house. Maybe it was because my father and I used to spend so much time there, playing classic games and talking smack. It felt like I had been gone much longer than I actually had.

I mused as I strolled, contemplating the internal shiftings I had noticed within myself. Attachment was something new for me. I cared about Asimov, *sure*, but I had his AI backed up daily to multiple hard-drives. With Allen, the connection felt so pressing, *urgent*.

The game room was on the left side of the hallway, framed in neon. I walked in, hearing the glorious sounds of gaming. All the crackles, compressed digital squelches—they made me nostalgic for a time long before my birth. That was always such an odd sensation—reflective, warm, yet alien—as though seeing someone else playing you in your dreams.

Allen's hair was wild and unkempt as he came into view, concentrating intensely on Blood—a retro FPS game I adored. The kid wasn't half bad, either. He did the 'pitchfork dance' exceptionally well with the zombies, using line-of-sight breaks to plan his assault room-by-room. I stood behind him, admiring his skill and the game itself silently for a while. Once he reached a level end screen, I said his name softly.

He jumped, his eyes bulging as he squealed. "Ah—oh. Leon. You scared me pretty bad," Al said, panting. I chuckled, responding, "I see that, kid. You were doing really well. That's one of my favorite games, and it's known for being insanely difficult. I'm impressed."

Allen beamed at my compliment, still panting from his jolt of fear. "Th-thank you," he said, grinning and regaining his composure. I nodded, smiling. "You're welcome. When you finish up, just give me a shout, okay?" He nodded dutifully, going back into the carnage for a while. As I stepped away, something in me snapped.

You run from that which could be your salvation, little Leon. If you miss your father so much—those gaming nights—and you walk away, you're walking away from giving Allen those same memories. Don't you ever grow weary of things just being the two of us?

Visions blurred by, a deluge of images, sights, sounds—and then I saw us. Us the way we used to be. Michael and Leon Crimson, quite the pair. We hunched over the Killer Instinct cabinet, beating one another's ass with potent ultra combos. Shouting gleefully, blind to all but the moment we were in. It was magic, beautiful, everything a young boy could hope to feel with his father. Then, the images ceased. I felt tears drenching my cheeks.

I wiped them away, grateful my back was turned to Allen. Why, all of a sudden, had the Daemon chosen to drive me for something *good*? He was an enigma, cruel, kind, seductive—because he was me. He was my dark-mind. And though it was easy to let neurotransmissions and poor mental chemistry steer the ship, at the end of the day—I was in control. Leon, not some faceless entity.

I stood frozen in the doorway of the games room. The bit-crushed wails of cultists being blasted and Caleb's one-liners beckoned me like a moth to flame. Turning, I had an excellent idea. I walked forth, and spoke. "If you like Blood, you should play Doom with me. We can play co-op."

"Really?!" Allen shrieked gleefully. I nodded, walking to a pc right next to his and seating myself. He promptly quit Blood and followed my instructions for setting up the Brutal Doom Mod and running a LAN game. By the time he and I had laid waste to the demons on E1M1, I could see that he was hooked. His grin could practically crack his face.

"This is so. Freaking. COOL!" he shouted, his fists balled in unfettered joy. I grinned at him, feeling the seed of love blooming in his presence. Allen was to be my salvation. I felt it, like Adam felt the draw to Eve in the garden. Each of us lets our serpent smooth-talk us into folly and ruin. But together, we could overcome the serpents, leviathans, and any other foolish creature that fell into our path.

For three hours, we blasted our way through demons, and came out victorious, the score card showing the results of our rampage. I felt the tension in my shoulders melt away as we were playing, and by the time we finished, I felt relaxed. Allen was grinning madly, like he had just gotten his Christmas presents early. Then, it hit me—Christmas was two months away. I had to get him *something*.

"Wash up for dinner, kid. We'll talk about something important then." He nodded, saying, "Yes, Leon. I'm sure it's gonna be great!" "I'm sure it will be," I said, smiling. "You're to help whenever you like with Asimov's cooking tasks. That's another gift you've got that I *fully* intend on using to my benefit," I chuckled, getting up and taking my leave.

* * *

At five o'clock, the delicious aroma of pasta and garlic bread greeted me from the kitchen. I sat at the dining table, nursing a White Russian in my silk robe, slippered feet propped on an extra chair. Father and Mother wouldn't have approved, but some habits never die.

"That is the most delectable bolognese I've seen!" Asimov said loudly to Allen in the kitchen. "No, really?" "Of course! Master Leon will be *most* pleased, I assure you. You've a gift, young Master Allen. It shall be an honor to observe your journey in all the things you enjoy." I smiled, listening to my best friends in the kitchen. At that moment, things felt almost complete. There was a missing piece, and most likely always would be.

In the grand scheme of things, it wasn't a massive piece. I hadn't felt so complete in most of my days upon the Stygian Hell I endured. For many people, this was as close to Heaven as it got. I sat in silence, soaking up the warm feelings that I had foregone for so long. Far too long.

"Dinner is served, sir!" Asy exclaimed as Allen and himself came out of the kitchen bearing our meal upon ornate silver serving trays. Steam billowed from the delectable mountain of pasta and rich meaty sauces. Gobs of a stringy mozzarella-provolone mixture bubbled hotly atop French Bread slathered in garlic-butter. My saliva instantly pooled, my stomach roaring in impatience.

Allen was beaming proudly, as he should be. "Have a seat, let's dig in," I told him with a smile. He obliged, sitting opposite me. Asimov plated each of us generous portions, then provided myself with a glass of Merlot and Allen, his now-ceremonial Dr. Pepper. The kid needed to gain weight. *I* would not stop him. I twirled the pasta onto my fork, my mouth watering.

Vince screamed, the dildo ripping his insides out with each thrust. My eyes sharpened, and I was back with my friends. I felt a panic attack brimming up, but could luckily fight it away. "How is it, Leon?" Allen asked, his face hopeful.

"It's the best I've ever had. No offense, Asy." "None taken, sir." He grinned, proud of what he had done. We continued on, laughing and feasting for a while. Once Allen and I were both leaning back in our chairs with full bellies, I decided it was time to get down to business. "Al?" "Yes, Leon?"

"Asimov has informed me you've met your end of the agreement. You gained weight. Are you still wanting to train?" His eyes bulged, hands blurring in excitement. Coherent words weren't what greeted my ears, but the message was clear—he wanted in. I laughed at his excited verbal onslaught, and we enjoyed our meal to the last bite. Tomorrow would be a big day—an end to wallowing, and a beginning of a new chapter. I hoped it'd be a good one.

X: 0500 Wake-up

Dawn blew her gilded trumpet, my alarm severing the deep, restful slumber I had been enjoying. It was time for Allen to see what it took to wear the mantle. What it took to do the things I do. I rose from the cool embrace of black, silken sheets, yawning as I performed my perfunctory wake-up stretch. Five a.m. —time to start the day.

I walked to my closet, donning black workout attire— sweatpants, breathable shirt, socks and running shoes. By the time I reached Allen's doorway, he jerked the door open, smiling at me with sleep still in his eyes. "Good morning," I said. "Mornin'." "Let's get to it. Drink plenty of water after dinner?" He nodded, and I led the way.

Allen and I made our way down the grand stairwell, taking the door at the end of the east wing's hallway outside. Early morning in Louisiana was thick, soupy, and hot. That applied whether it was winter or summer, it seemed. I took the lead, running us through stretches and a light warm-up of jumping jacks. Once our blood was flowing, I let him catch his breath as I ran over the details of our workout.

"We're going to conduct a four-mile run, followed by an upper-body regiment. Tomorrow, we will do the same, only swapping for abdominals and legs. Sunday is our recuperation day. Two hundred repetitions per exercise is the standard. That can be all at once, or broken into sets. Do you think you can handle it?" Allen's eyes looked fearful, but eager. He slowly nodded, and I patted him on the back. He was going to do just fine.

For the first mile, he held on and hung tough. By mile three, however, all the pasta that hadn't digested yet spewed on the running track. I let him retch, handing him a bottle of water. Once he was good, we resumed. All-in-all, he did really well for his first day. He finished the run and did push-ups and dips until he hit muscle failure. That was more than enough for me—I just needed to see a concerted effort on his end.

The first week rolled by, Allen struggling, but showing heart throughout every workout. By Sunday, the boy was beat. He could barely keep his eyes open at the dinner table. In fact, at one point, Asimov caught his head just before the kid waterboarded himself in a bowl of French onion soup. I felt a twinge of guilt, wondering whether I was pushing him too hard.

By the second week, he was becoming strong. Incredibly strong. He couldn't keep my pace yet, but he didn't stop at any point for our four-mile run. No vomit, which I was grateful for. He knocked out one hundred and sixty reps per exercise before hitting muscle failure. I was proud, and watching him grow and adapt was inspiring.

On the Sunday evening of the second week, we enjoyed a lasagna for our carb-load. Allen and Asimov had again produced five star food, my mouth watering at the sight of all that cheese, beef, Italian sausage steaming in gooey mounds. After making my customary (but always genuine) compliments on the food, and felt that maybe Allen was closer to readiness for firearm training than initially projected. His arms had taken on muscle mass—lean and toned, but strong.

A formerly gaunt face had filled out—hell, he was almost within the weight range that was ideal for his age. Once he hit one hundred pounds, I felt he could handle the physical aspect weapons training. Safety would be paramount, of course. I would go over firearm safety in great detail prior to handing him anything in my armory.

"What are you thinking about, Leon?" Allen asked, his strong brown eyes directly on mine. I snapped out of my inner thoughts and felt a bit of surprise. Al was growing—comfortable around me. I savored the thought before speaking. "Well, kid—I'm thinking about your progress so far. Frankly, I'm astonished with what you've accomplished." He blushed, waving my words away and saying, "I couldn't even do all the reps the first week. I haven't hit two hundred yet, and-"

"Hush, kid. The workout we're doing would put many grown men on their ass. And besides, this has been to get you healthy, but it's also been to see how badly you want to do the work I do. I won't be able to let you do it in good conscience without seeing that you're physically and mentally capable. You've proven that you are, in spades. So cast aside all those doubts. I'm proud of you."

For a while, Allen simply smiled and sat silently. I saw a tiny tear trickle down his face, which he hastily wiped away, pretending to have an itch. "Thank you," he whispered, lifting a bite of cheesy pasta to his mouth. "You're welcome. Well, keep at it. Firearm training will require discipline, and so far,

I'm liking what I'm seeing."

We finished that meal, smiling and idly talking about what game we should play next. After a long and arduous council, we ran through some Duke Nukem 3D. We played for hours, laughing at one-liners and finding secrets. Nighttime came, and we each went to bed. It was a good day.

* * *

A month and a half later, and we were moving as a unit. We flew through our run, and our muscle training. The kid barely broke a sweat anymore, and his age was finally showing now that he had packed some healthy weight on. I couldn't have been any more proud of him. What had been a malnourished little boy in a concrete hell was now a growing young man. He would be stronger than me—I felt it in my bones.

After showering, we had the rest of the day to enjoy. My feelers on the dark web had uncovered panic in PCP after my little fireworks display. I had hurt them, wiped away their bread and butter. Good. Let the cunts bleed financially. I'd bleed them physically soon enough.

While showering, a brilliant idea came to mind. Although I seldom left the house, a change of scenery might do the boy some good. Asimov could use a break from cooking. I had some upgrades for him that would take time to implement. Crimson Manor was about to rapidly shift from a solitary lair to a fortified compound. The stakes were higher with every passing day.

Stepping out of the shower, I toweled off while looking in the mirror. My puffy eyes were sharp—the eyes of an apex predator. The physical regiment and sleep had done wonders for my health. I realized in that moment that I had had no substance other than my one glass of wine in the evening for over a week.

You're getting back to the killer you were born to be, little Leon. Now you must go forth and take back your life. Show Vurisberg that it hasn't broken you yet. The time to kill will come again—and soon. Enjoy this.

I rolled my eyes at my dark-mind's ramblings—pick a fucking lane. All I knew was that I felt good, and Allen deserved a treat for all his hard work. I dressed, choosing a simple black suit with a charcoal gray tie. After all our endeavors, we deserved something delicious and a day off. It's good to throw yourself a bone from time to time.

By the time I had reached the first floor, sounds of Brutal Doom drifted to me from the east wing. Allen had it cranked, and was well into E2M3 by the sounds of it. I left him to it, paging Asimov on my watch. He promptly arrived, eager to serve, as always. "Yes, Master Leon? How may I help you?"

"Asy, I'd like for you to pick somewhere for Allen and I to eat. Make it a surprise. No Italian, since I've been carb-loading us to death as is," I said, chuckling. Asy matched, his digital imitation truly adorable to me in that moment. Fuck, *where* had all these good feelings come from? Was this how *normal* people felt every day? Must be nice.

"Yes, sir. Is there anything else I can do for you?" I nodded, patting his cold steel 'shoulder,' out of force of habit. "Actually, I have something I want to do for *you*, my man. You have a new series of upgrade modules ready for you. When you finish your daily list, go to your pod."

"That's most exciting, sir! I shall use them to their maximum effect." I nodded, and let him go off to continue his list of tasks. Allen was still blasting away in the game room. "If you can't beat 'em, join 'em," I said to myself with a smirk. We beat the game together, and by the time we were done, dinner time was nearing.

"Let's go out, kid. Sound good?" I asked as I rose from the desk. Allen hopped up, excited and grinning. "It sure does! Where are we going?" "That's the good part—I told Asimov to surprise us. Let's go eat. No PT tomorrow." With those words, the boy was ecstatic. He began raving over how much gaming he was going to do later. I grinned at him, leading the way to the garage. "Wowwwww," Al breathed next to me, staring at the fifty-plus collection of hover cars.

"Shit, kid. I forgot you hadn't been to this part of the property yet," I said with a grin. "Which one do you want to take out? Try not to take too long to pick, we have about thirty minutes to reach the restaurant." He took off like a bullet, eyeing the line of mechanical muscle at our disposal. "This one!" he shouted excitedly.

It was a Lamborghini Z-666, top-of-the-line Italian muscle. Sharp angles in a translucent crimson finish. Even then, the sight of it took my breath away. Unbeknownst to Allen, he had chosen my favorite car. I loved him even more at that moment.

We hopped into the car, and I engaged the grav-thrusters. It levitated smoothly, the engine and propulsion system humming powerfully. Al was grinning ear-to-ear, his hands patting his lap frantically. "Let's beat it, kid," I said, powering the accelerator up and zooming out of the complex. On the speakers, the lead-laden riffs of Black Sabbath blared.

XI: Sonnet

On the Northside, GPS brought us to a fast food establishment. I laughed, despite myself. I had told Asy to surprise me. It was themed like a drive-in from the nineteen-fifties, adorned in multicolored rods of neon. Admittedly, it smelled incredible, and I could tell Allen was excited.

"Ever been to a Sonnet before?" I asked, watching his reaction. He shook his head silently, and I felt a surge of shame. That question lacked any foresight, given what I knew about Allen's life prior. "Well, it's pretty damn good, I can tell you that much. Chicken tenders, burgers, hot dogs, mozzarella sticks—it'll definitely help us bulk you up more." He looked a little embarrassed, and said, "I don't know what any of that is, except for chicken tenders."

I grinned, waving away his concern. I pressed a button on the order stall's display, and moments later was greeted by a sweet voice. "Welcome to Sonnet, Veronica speaking! How may I help you today?" Something in her energy was infectious—it was the genuine *kindness* laden into it. Most people would sound half-dead doing that line of work, and do—given my brief encounters with them over the years.

"Yes, Veronica—I know this is going to sound ridiculous, but—I'd like two of everything, please." A moment of silence stretched out before she tentatively asked if I was pulling a prank. It was a fair question. I laughed, responding, "No, Veronica, it's no prank. My recently adopted family has never had anything from Sonnet. We're going to feast like kings."

Sweet, sunshiny rays of laughter came through the speakers. I could hear a faint note of relief. "Okay, sounds like *I* need to get adopted by your family, as well. Your total will be $287.32. It'll be a small wait, I hope that's not a problem." "Not a problem at all," I said while grinning. I scanned my card to pay, and we awaited our impending mountain of food.

* * *

I was starved in ways I never contemplated before I laid eyes on her, my dusky queen with flowing tangles of ebony curls that framed a gorgeous moon-shaped face. Veronica had two loaded down trays of steaming hot food, but all I could look at was *her*. I hastily stepped out to help her load the food into the trunk compartment. On level ground, I realized how compact she was, and I loved it. Although I only stand at five foot eight, I towered over her.

"Thanks, Veronica. I hope they've been treating you well here," I said politely. "They know better than to *not* treat me well," she said with a fierce grin on her face. Soulful, dark eyes like embers bore into mine.

Little Leon, don't you tire of doing this thing alone? Wouldn't it be nice to grab a pretty face and fuck it? Doesn't revenge-raping pedophiles get fucking old?

It did, but that act wasn't for me. It was for my foes to witness in fear. Daemon grew quiet, but his message lingered. Veronica delicately placed the last brown paper bag loaded with food into the trunk, and I stopped her before she left. "Let me tip you. You've been excellent," I said.

Veronica graciously halted her exit, appearing grateful before I even pulled a $100 bill from my wallet. She took the bill gently, and when her finger grazed mine, I felt a magnetically induced compulsion to touch her again. "Thank you so much, sir!" She turned, and as she left, I blurted out, "Can I give you my number?"

It was *far* from my best pickup line. In my defense, I'm not exactly the 'pickup' type. Why work for it when you can buy a whore or fuck a severed head, right? But this connection was so serendipitously perfect—a restaurant picked at random by Asy—a beautiful woman with a kind soul that shined through—I had no choice. Veronica looked me up and down, a smirk on her face. "I think I can get behind that," she said, playfully biting her lip and letting her curly hair swing.

"I'm honored. Here's my card. Leon, by the way," I said, extending my hand for a shake. She gently shook my hand, taking my card with a grin. "One thing, Leon—if I text you, I better get a response. Unless you pick up *all* the girls at fast-food joints."

"Not recently," I said with a mirthful grin. Veronica laughed, putting her hand on my arm. There it was. It was all flowing. She and I said our goodbye's, and I took Allen back home. The food was delicious, make no mistake. My thoughts of her beneath me in my oh-so-empty king-sized bed were far more delectable. I lay in the dark, realizing I was in over my head, and probably didn't stand a chance. Sleep gradually took hold.

* * *

The following morning, I awoke painfully on my stomach with a rock-hard cock under me. I've always been a sexual being—as most are—but this was going to get out of hand if I didn't purge this aching lust. I checked my watch through groggy, sleep-laden eyes. When I saw Veronica's name on a notification, my pulse rose.

All the time I had spent putting moon roofs in pedophile skulls had dulled my game. I was in over my head—completely helpless.

Veronica: So, I've decided I like the look of you. Let's meet somewhere and have a coffee! I love Better Off Read. Meet me there at 5. Sound good?

Leon: Sounds great! I'll see you there!

I rose from my bed with what could only be described as a shit-eating grin. My cock swung majestically as I stretched, hard with the morning's supply. I got dressed, contemplating the risks of public exposure. A compact pistol and wrist-piercer would work just fine. It would be a facetious show of naivete to go unarmed *anywhere* in Vurisberg. Despite all I knew, I hoped Veronica and I could get to know one another undisturbed as I buttoned up my black dress shirt.

The color for the day was all black. People can say what they want—there is no sexier color. After tweaking my tie to perfection in the mirror, I slicked my hair back with a dab of pomade. In just twenty minutes, I had transformed from a half-comatose goblin with morning wood to a handsome billionaire. A little effort can truly go a long way.

Nodding approval in the mirror, I excitedly made my way downstairs. Asimov was surely about, and I wanted to lay eyes on his upgrades before I departed. I paged him with my watch, and he arrived shortly afterwards. Cosmetically, Asy looked no different. That was perfect—I needed him to appear helpless.

"Good morning, sir! How might I assist you?" he asked. I patted his forearms, saying, "Let me see those upgrades, Asy. I want to make sure the pod installed them properly." He promptly rotated his hands right, and a panel slid out of the way—the arm-mounted .45 mini-gun attachments no longer concealed. I let out an enthusiastic whistle, surveying the hardware and checking for any imperfections in their installation.

"Damn fine addition, eh?" I asked with a grin. Asimov nodded. "It shall make contributing to the safety of Crimson Manor an effortless affair. Thank you, Master Leon." "Don't mention it. That helps all of us. More security never hurts. Okay, that's good. Make sure Allen has a fun day today. I have a date, so I will be gone for a while."

"A date, sir? Are you pulling a prank on me?" "Watch it, wise-ass. And no. I'm as shocked as you," I said while cheesing like a buffoon. He took my instructions, assuring me that Al would be well-fed and provided any entertainment he requested. "That's perfect. I've got time to kill. I'll be at the range. It would be embarrassing for Allen's shooting instructor to miss, now wouldn't it?"

"Yes, sir. A tragedy beyond measure." "I'll kick your ass," I jeered playfully. After making my way to the armory, I chose an M-16 and twenty magazines of .556. The range was indoors on the west wing. Although the cost was ridiculous, it was completely soundproofed, with state-of-the-art pop-up targets that emitted blood squibs on impact. Given my complete lack of guests, I had converted four bedroom suites into an altar to lead and gunpowder. The range was optimized for up to one hundred and fifty meter engagements—optimal for most weapon ranges.

I stood at the firing position, and an automated voice counted down from ten. By one, I had the rifle raised, cocked and on fire. The thirty-five meter target popped down instantly, artificial blood splattering from the 'head' of the silhouette target. By my fourth magazine, I was warmed up and no longer missing any shots. Just to be safe, I fired through the remaining sixteen magazines. My accuracy rating read ninety-three percent on a display mounted on a wall. "Still got it," I said to myself with a grin.

The day dragged by as I awaited our date. Allen cheered loudly in the game room, clearly delving into another video game from a dead era. It felt good to not only preserve slices of history, but hand them down. I felt fortunate to have *anyone* to share my passions with. Grinning, I made my way into the game room. We ran through Doom 2, and by then it was time for me to head out.

"I'll be back later tonight or tomorrow morning, Al. Asy will assist you with anything you need." I said as I rose from the gaming desk. He nodded absentmindedly, fully immersed in the carnage on screen. I smiled, making my way to the garage. The hard part was on—choosing the vehicle for our first date.

XII: A Night On the Town

The wailing of the damned walking the sidewalks was but background noise for me as I sped through the streets of Vurisberg. I hardly even noticed the shootings, robbings, killings—getting to Veronica was all that was on my mind. Sewerslvt blared over my system, the bass booming and synths sounding larger than life. My cock had announced his return to the land of the living, and the rush of blood was euphoric.

Some things—the small ones, the seemingly insignificant ones—take a person back to when things were simpler. The combination of giddiness and arousal was like falling through a vortex back into my adolescence. As I drove, I pondered on what had changed for me as time cruelly lurched forwards. In the end, it was clear as day—trauma had fucked me up. That, and my psychosis began slipping free of its captivity around the time I was thirty.

According to my GPS, Better Off Read was a book/coffee shop in Northside. Crime reports were fairly promising for the five-block radius. Only four murders had occurred within the

70

vicinity over the past year. That was incredibly low. "Hopefully, our luck stays," I said to myself, speeding through the concrete hell I called home. Within ten minutes, I pulled up to the store and parked.

The store's sign was a masterclass in branding; a steaming cup of coffee accompanied skulls and crossbones. The font was like what early death metal bands used to use. I had to give it to Veronica—the place looked interesting. I felt I might even be inclined to grab a book while in there. Getting back into reading couldn't hurt. If nothing else, it could have been a useful distraction while sorting myself out.

Espresso's rich bouquet greeted my senses before I had even opened the door. I stepped in, instantly feeling out of place. Everyone was beautiful, alternative, and *niche.* And there I stood—primped up, dressed like a CEO with a stupid grin on my face that I couldn't seem to push away. Faint synth music played, the red lights swooning like an ethereal chamber of smoke across that temple to dark fiction. My eyes surveyed the shelves as I idly walked through. Every book was extreme to one extent or another, and it had me excited.

I picked up a random book off a shelf, purely on merit of its cover. "All the Rage," by David Hardy. The reds and blacks, the primal image of a man roaring out his fury—it was beautiful. I kept it in my hand, perusing more. Around me, beautiful people flitted by, conversing, drinking coffee, flipping through morbid and macabre tomes from an era of literature before our time. Sometimes, the things we love the most have been hidden behind the curtains of time past.

The rich aroma of Nag Champa incense soothed my soul as I looked through the massive array of books. My eyes scanned the roaming patrons, and there she was—Veronica. She had a book called "Talia," by Daniel J. Volpe in her hands, and her expression as she read was intoxicating. I could see arousal, disgust, giddy nervousness on her face as her eyes zoomed across the pages like a space shuttle departing the atmosphere.

I was gawking when she looked up at me. She didn't recoil, but grinned. "Hey, good looking," she said with a warm smile. "Hey, nice place here," I dumbly responded. "Oh, it's the *best!*," she squealed, clutching the paperback to her heart as her eyes lit up. "They have all the splatterpunk you can read, and even do," she lowered her voice, leaning close to whisper, "they do small batch pressings for new stuff. But you didn't hear that from me."

I couldn't help but smile, listening to her as she ran me through the intricacies of a genre I had never heard of before. When she said the word 'gore', my dick flooded with blood, standing taut against the fabric of my slacks. Her eyes flitted downwards, but she said nothing. Her smile grew, and the energy intensified as we spoke.

She definitely saw it. And she wants it. Let it roll, little Leon. Let it roll.

"What kind of coffee would you like?" I asked, eager to get some espresso into my system. "Double double, please," she said sweetly, her eyes darting back down to her book. "Sure thing," I said, making my way to the coffee bar. A striking goth-mommy type was working the counter. I ordered Veronica's double-double, and an iced mocha for myself with an extra shot of espresso. I paid, and when the drinks were ready, I headed over to a small circular table with chairs. She sat directly beside me, leaning her head against my shoulder as she read.

"Thank you," she said dreamily, her chapter nearing an end. I nodded and caught a waft of her hair. It smelled clean and looked so soft. *Sure would be nice to get a grip of it and bury your cock to its hilt in her throat, eh?* I ignored the Daemon's prodding, although there was some truth to the taunts. Veronica put the book down, taking a cautious sip of her coffee and looking at me in interest.

"Leon, I'm enjoying this. But I have to ask—what made you want to go after *me*?" Without missing a beat, I let the truth flow. "First, it was your voice, your energy. You were kind to a stranger in a line of work that can be so...soul crushing. Then—I saw you. It didn't take much more than that for me. I know I'm being forward," I said, grinning as my face flushed the slightest amount. "It's forward, but—I'm the kind of girl who doesn't mind forward," she said with a lascivious grin. I felt her hand under the table, drawing circles on my upper thigh, then gripping my erection through my pants, stroking the thick shaft softly.

I let a small gasp escape, my pleasure center activating and testosterone beginning to boil. Veronica's blazing eyes bore into mine, our lust brooding. This instant attraction was primal, beyond reproach. I wanted to feel her from the inside. I wanted to make her scream for her new god in silk sheets with a plug in her ass.

"Well, Leon, this is me. If I like you, I'll fuck you. I don't like bullshit or lies. I just want to have a good time, be honest, and get good dick. Can you handle that?" she asked, her voice becoming laden in shimmering sex. "I can. I can definitely handle that," I said, my throat dry and voice crackling from all the building tension in my loins. "Good," she cooed, her thumb rocking back and forth over the ridge of my glans, my pleasure skyrocketing.

Mercifully, she stopped playing with my dick. I could feel my face burning, my breath catching. Looking around, it seemed no one had noticed our brief incursion. The fact that they could have seen it turned me on more. I drowned in a tidal wave of arousal.

"So," she said, letting her voice fall back to her normal, bubbly one, "what do you want to do after we get ourselves some books?" I pondered the question for a moment. "I figured we'd grab a bite, if that's alright with you." "That sounds good! Anything in particular you want to eat?" I leaned forward, feeling a smirk growing. She started this.

"How about you, spread eagle and bound to my poster bed?" I asked, feeling my heat rising, my libido ascending to its Emperor's throne. "Well, I meant before we get to brass tacks," she teased, her smile turning me on that much more. It felt good to have this connection—and I didn't want it to stop. Veronica paused, contemplating where we'd be dining. Her brow furrowed and lips pursed as she went deep in thought. It was quite a cute look, if I'm being honest.

"I know!" she exclaimed, promptly snatching my phone and inputting an address into the GPS. "Don't look," she demanded, her eyes fiery while she grinned madly. "I won't," I promised, cheesing like a moron. We sat in comfortable silence, savoring our coffees and flipping through the books we'd grabbed. By the sixth page, I knew I'd grabbed a winner.

"I take it, you're liking that one?" she asked, eyeing me curiously. I nodded affirmation, saying, "It's fast-paced and mean. Who wouldn't?" Apparently that was an appropriate answer, because Veronica was staring me down like a nice, fresh cut of steak. "Grab the sequel, 'Consumed' while you're at it, then! You'll be glad you did." "I will! In fact, why don't you load us each up a basket. Recommendations for me, and anything you'd like for yourself."

"Are you serious?!" she squealed joyously. The moment I nodded to confirm, she shot off, ping-ponging around the store as she grabbed seemingly every book that wasn't nailed down. I couldn't help but grin, watching her excitement and unadulterated joy. She was a woman who knew what she wanted, and didn't require the world to find happiness. *You're already wrapped, you silly little bitch.*

I shook away the Daemon's taunting, and simply enjoyed the moment for what it was. Ten minutes later, Veronica came back to me at our table with roughly forty books. Her eyes were wide—*alive.* It was both adorable, scary, and incredibly *sexy* to me.

"That everything?" I joked. "It is. But I'm warning you—this genre becomes a lifelong addiction. Nothing will ever be the same after. Can you handle that?" I chuckled, but I could tell she was dead serious. "Yes, ma'am. I can handle much more than you'd probably expect." "We shall see," she teased, setting the baskets on the tabletop.

I rose, grabbing the book baskets and getting in line for the register. Veronica stood beside me, her head laid upon my shoulder. The tropical scent of her dark hair was driving me wild. We lurched forwards in the line, beautiful goth people surrounding us—buying books and going about their lives. It was oddly serene, and then we arrived at the register.

The man working the counter was unlike anyone I'd laid eyes upon before. His eyes were solid black, crimson hair pulled into a topknot, with sharpened teeth. Every exposed inch of his pale skin was covered in tattoos—satanic symbols, Latin, and Baphomet peeking from under his tank top. "Thank you for shopping Better Off Read. I hope you could find everything easily," he hissed behind his fangs.

"Oh, we did!" Veronica said in a bubbly voice, beaming as we placed the books upon the register. I glanced at the strange man's nameplate—Stuart. He grinned, his eyes unreadable portals to the void. If nothing else, he was fast, ringing our forty-three book spree up in less than five minutes. "Your total will be six hundred, sixty-six dollars, sir," he said with a maniacal grin.

Without a thought, I tapped my transfer fob to the receiver. It beeped, the transaction approved instantly. Veronica danced in place by my side as I grabbed the bags, nodding thanks. We made our way outside, Veronica's modest hover car parked across from mine. It was sleek gray, with a 'Support Indie Authors' bumper sticker. She was a woman behind her principles—something that only made me want her more.

"This is my ride. I'll take my books," she said, only grabbing three books from the heap. Her grin at me was mischievous, utterly adorable in every conceivable way. After lovingly placing her copies in her trunk, she followed me to my car. I loaded my newfound library into the trunk, watching her expression for any clue of what I was getting myself into.

"Are you gonna stand there checking me out all day, or are we going to eat?" she teased. "I suppose we eat. Does it have to be a surprise?" Veronica's nose crinkled at me. "Do you want it to be any fun? Of course it has to be a surprise! Now, get behind the wheel." Who was I to argue? I slid into the driver's seat, engaging the grav thrusters as she checked her makeup in the mirror. It was perfect, of course—just enough to highlight the natural beauty she already held.

GPS booted up over the audio system, giving step-by-step instructions. In the close quarters of my car, her sweet smells were maddening. She was delicious in so many ways, and the thought of tearing those clothes off and exploring her curves with my tongue was all-consuming. We drove towards the slower part of town, where pedestrians dragging hopeless feet diminished to almost no one. Abandoned plants replaced run-down convenience stores and adult shops. There was hardly a prostitute in sight—the true sign we were in no-man's-land.

At last, GPS ordered us to park. Looking around, I felt a prank was being played. We sat parked before a dingy, rust-spotted warehouse. It loomed, derelict and ominous, leaves tumbling across a crack-riddled parking lot. "Are you fucking with me?" I asked incredulously. If she was about to call in the hounds to jump me, I was grateful I had my wrist launcher on. She began laughing, wheezing behind her hand as mirthful tears streamed her face.

"Calm down, tough guy. Just trust, okay?" I paused, scrutinizing her, reading her, scanning for threats. There was none—just a beautiful woman laughing at me for being so damn paranoid. Relieved (if still on guard), I got out of the car, walking around and letting her out. "What a gentleman," she said between gales of laughter. Veronica took my hand, leading me to the entrance of the warehouse. Once we were near the front door, the delicious aroma of Italian greeted me.

"This is my favorite place. If you love horror, it'll become yours, too," she said, opening the door for me. I walked into a place unknown, nervous, but ready for whatever surprises the night had in store. Whatever questions I had were answered when I saw the cardboard cutout of Art, the Clown near the entrance. It was a 'Terrifier' themed Italian restaurant. I began cackling at the absurdity of my trepidation. Veronica joined in, patting my back.

A hostess dressed as a victim took us to our seats, her prosthetic wounds ghastly and fascinating. She seated us at a table designed to look covered in filth and rust. It was just a simple stencil job, but quite effective from a distance. I was in awe of the attention to detail spent upon the restaurant. As I took my seat, I looked at Veronica and saw her eager anticipation. "This place is pretty great! I thought I was the only person who still enjoyed media from the last century. Terrifier is a great body horror flick," I said.

She responded to my remark with a happy squeal. She had her hands clasped, bouncing in place as she celebrated. "I'm *so* glad you said that. Look at the menus! They all have punny names. It's fucking adorable!" she exclaimed, her eyes deeply cast into mine. Perusing the menu, I had a chuckle at the item names: Slut Slaughter Spaghetti, Laceration Lasagna, Cut-up Cunt Carrot Cake. This was *my* kind of place.

Chains hung from iron beams, and fake blood splattered everywhere. Mock intestines dangled about in random spots. Overall, it was a beautiful mock-up for the warehouse featured in the film. Our server stalked up, Art the clown (albeit a convincing cosplay). Veronica giggled madly, clapping and watching my face for a reaction.

Art didn't speak, of course, only gestured comically at the menu and shrugged. I chuckled as his murderous dark eyes stared into mine. "I'll have the Laceration Lasagna, please. With a coke," I said politely. Art's gaze shifted to Veronica, who bounced joyously. "Oooooh! I'll have the Carnage Chicken Alfredo, extra chicken! And a coke." With that, Art bowed his pale head, walking away to place our orders.

"The food here is *soooo* good! I'm glad you didn't bail before we came inside. Vibe check, passed," she said with a wink. All I could do was smile, grateful I hadn't pulled out my firearm in panic. Going out as Leon never felt safe. Without my moniker, I felt vulnerable. Those feelings were subsiding in her presence, however. Something about her—felt like home.

I gazed upon her across the table. Her energy was brimming and infectious. By the time our dinner came out, my mouth was already watering. The plates lovingly loaded in generous portions of delectable pasta, garnished with basil. Veronica wasted no time in scooping up a hearty bite of noodle and meat. Sauce lightly spattered on her chin as she slurped the noodle, dancing in place. When she noticed me watching, she only moved more vivaciously and took another bite.

"If you can't beat 'em, join 'em, I suppose," I said, digging into my meal. An involuntary moan escaped from the bite—it was the best lasagna I'd ever had. I'd never tell Asy or Allen, of course, but—holy fuck, it was something *else*. Neither of us said a word after our first bites. We ate until our plates were clean and our stomachs ached. I paid with my fob as we walked out, tipping twenty-five percent. I knew walking around in prosthetics and makeup all day like that had to be hard work.

"Fuck, I'm stuffed," she said, rubbing her tummy contentedly as she walked beside me, her head nestled against my shoulder. I was mid-response, when a sketchy bunch converged from the shadows, surrounding us in that destitute parking lot. They all wore red cloth masks, crowbars in their hands. "Can I help you?" I asked with a layer of false calm. Inside, my drills and training were taking over. You don't get second chances in a world like this.

"Yeah. You can start by handing over the bitch. Then, everything of value you've got. Including the ride."

I fought to keep my exterior calm, blocking their line of

sight with Veronica. "I'm afraid I can't abide by any of that, gentlemen. This may be one you don't want to start," I said, growling by the end. I didn't have the patience for this shit. *I'm fucking Spiritcrusher.*

"Ha! This rich little pussyboy thinks he's about to *do* someth-" one thug began before my wrist launcher made quick work of him. A six-inch blade had severed his carotid arteries, embedding into the spinal cord. Blood gushed and flowed, and as the hostiles realized the situation they were in, I raised my wrist again, flicking it to the side. Another down, gulping for air and gargling in his blood. "Take cover behind a car. Move!" I commanded Veronica, who hastily obeyed with wide eyes.

In the chaos of the impending bloodbath, I had time to draw my .45 from its concealed holster. I aimed true, squeezing the trigger in rapid succession as I cycled my targets. They lay about my feet, bleeding, brained, lobotomized. Good fucking riddance. I spat upon their corpses. "Fucking trash," I growled.

A lightning bolt of realization flashed through the blood-thirsty haze I was in. Veronica. This had ruined everything. Turning, I expected to see her frightened or running away. Instead, her eyes locked with mine. I was her prey, she my huntress. "Are you okay?" I asked, walking over to her. She said nothing, only grasped my face and drew my lips to hers.

Our kiss was a landfall—an explosion of thermal fissures—with the force of trains colliding. She was everything; her taste all consuming in my mouth. "Yeah, I'm good. Let's get out of here," she said in a breathy, enthralled voice. We hopped in the car, lifting and speeding away into the night. I heard her panting in the passenger seat, adrenaline still surging her system. "That was—not how I wanted things to go. I understand if you don't want to see me again after this," I said through clenched teeth, my heart already aching at the thought.

"I want to see you. I want to see all of you, right now," she said. Glancing over, our eyes locked, and I burnt to a husk in that vortex of animalistic lust. The fires of passion burned exponentially hotter with every passing second together. "Can we get your car and head to my place? I'd really like a shower," I said, doing my best to smirk coolly. "A shower sounds perfect," Veronica cooed. When we arrived back at Better Off Dead, I input my address for her.

"I'll see you soon," I said.

"I can't wait."

We pulled out of the lot, heading to Crimson Manor. My dick throbbed, pre-cum oozing onto my leg as I drove. I had wanted nothing this badly in forever. I was going to make the most of it.

Chapter XIII: Deep

When I arrived at the gates, I paged Asimov using my watch. "Yes, sir? How may I be of service?" "Hey Asy, make sure Allen's in bed. I have a guest, and—discretion is best, right?" "Oh, you *scoundrel*. It shall be done, sir. Your bed is made with fresh linens, and an extra robe is in the guest bathroom." I grinned, appreciating my android friend's faith in my ability to seal the deal.

"I have her vehicle scanned under 'safe', so just direct her to the guest bathroom, if you don't mind. Thanks, Asimov. Out." With that, I pulled around the side of the house, parking in my garage. With a racing heart, I made my way inside, walking on air all the way to my master suite. I stripped in the bathroom, chucking my clothes into the laundry chute before setting the water temperature. Once it was steaming, I stepped in.

You've gotten yourself quite a pretty catch, little Leon. Enjoy this night, for time's cruel curtain closes at a time of its own volition. I ignored the Daemon's dribble, lathering up my body as I stared at the ceiling. The tension in my muscles was at an all-time high, my heart a thunderous drumroll. I slowly focused on my breathing, doing slow cycles to steady my mind as hot water blasted away the blood from my encounter.

A sudden pressure on my shoulder and change of temperature caused my fight instincts to kick in, muscles tensing and fists clenched. Veronica giggled behind me, and I let the tension go. "You didn't think I was showering *alone*, did you?" she asked, smiling lustfully. I let out a low chuckle as she began kissing the nape of my neck, soft hands running across my hot, wet skin.

The soft, delicate sensations were so intimate. I let out a contented sigh, leaning my face forwards and pulling her tight against my back by her arms. She kissed from my neck down my shoulders, then grabbed me gently by the head and turned me to face her. Her eyes scorched deeply into my soul, and our mouths collided. Scalding water drenched us, my tongue swirling deliciously with hers, a fistful of her thick, dark hair.

My body pressed against hers—she was velvet lava. I needed to be incinerated. "What you did back there was so fucking *hot*," she hissed through teeth clenched in lust. My cock engorged, brushing against her soft skin. Without a moment's hesitation, she grabbed it, slowly and lovingly stroking my length as she kissed me deeply.

"I—I was worried I had scared you away," I admitted, moaning with her slow and loving motions. "You did the opposite. But, I have to ask—who are you, *really*?"

There it was. The moment I had dreaded for a later time dropped at my doorstep. Upon reflection, I don't think Batman ever admitted his secret identity while being jerked off in a shower. It's been a magically unexpected journey, my life.

"What do you mean? I'm Leon," I said, smirking. I knew the

jig was up. Veronica wasn't dumb, and I was pretty sure she wouldn't give up, now that she wanted to know something. "Yes, you're Leon. But I don't know many men in business suits who can drop six armed men in less than a minute. So, be honest with me, please. Who are you?" Her eyes set on mine, unwavering and unfaltering.

No time like the present. Shit or get off the pot.

"Can you keep a secret?" I asked, my tone shifting to the hue of a vortex. Veronica's eyes locked with mine as she nodded slowly, her hand still delicately stroking me. "Promise me." I pinned her against the shower wall, my hand on her throat as I bit her lip. After a moment, I loosened my grip so she could speak.

"Cross my heart, and hope to die," she said in a breathy whisper. "Good. I'm Spiritcrusher," I said, stepping back and watching her reaction. "It all adds up," she said thoughtfully. "Okay, thank you for telling me. Now I'm much more willing to stay the night." Veronica winked at me, stepping forward and kissing me deeply. Although I was taken aback by how little she seemed affected, the *now* was screaming for me to get out of my head, for once.

My hands explored her soft and ample curves as our tongues swirled, and my lust roared darkly. She was intoxicating—purer than Colombian whites fresh off the ship. Our moans intermingled, dancing primally and echoing as I gently tweaked and rubbed her nipples. I continued kissing her as she reached for body wash and began to massage and lather up my body. She started at my tense shoulders, her hands firm and worshipful.

The gorgeous brown of her skin popped on my paleness, her fingers expert and caring in their touch. We washed one another, kissing the entire time. "You deserve a reward for today, Daddy," she cooed, rubbing circles on the tip of my cock with her thumb in lazy revolutions. "Yeah?" I asked in a breathy moan. "Yeah, dry up and lay out on the bed. You're not worrying about a *thing*," she said, her face sincere and hypnotic.

I gladly obliged, stepping out of the shower and toweling off. All the blood in my body had concentrated in my cock, which throbbed achingly for more of her touch. Although it was near impossible, I walked away from her to the poster bed and laid out upon black silk sheets that smelled of fabric softener. The sheets were an icy palm upon my hot skin, the gentle rustle of the fabric soothing to my ears.

Veronica walked into the room, my dark conqueror, her skin shining and hair lustrous. "Do you have—bindings?" she asked meaningfully, staring me down like her next feast. "I do. They're in the nightstand." She walked over, pulling out ties still in their packaging. A sad look crossed her face for a moment. "You never got to use these?" "No, most of my sex is of the revenge variety. Bindings are to prevent escape when I use them," I said.

"Why do you think *I* use them?" she teased, quickly tying my first wrist and anchoring it to a post on the bed. In less than five minutes, I was nude and sprawled in binds on a vast bed with a hungry woman holding me at her mercy. *This is as close to Heaven as it gets for someone like you, little Leon.* For once, the Daemon and I were singing the same tune.

Veronica gently crawled towards me atop the bed, her eyes never leaving mine. She straddled my stomach, leaning down and kissing me as her fingers ran through my hair. Underneath the veil of lust, something else was stirring as our skin melded and her pulse raced with mine. It must have shown through my eyes, because she kissed me deeper, holding my face like something precious she didn't dare drop.

"You're mine now. I'll take care of you," she said between kisses. I submitted fully to her, then. She slid down, kissing my neck, then shoulders. Her lips were soft, inviting, her kisses firm and hot. I sighed contentedly, my skin prickling from the electricity between us. She giggled softly as she made her way lower and lower, her lips dragging down my body, hot breath causing a chilling wave to crash over me.

No one looked as beautiful as her, my throbbing dick in her hand, oozing pre-cum and aching to fill every hole she'd offer me. My aching need was a constant wail, and her lusty gaze drove me mad. Veronica smiled sweetly, laying on her stomach and gripping my manhood at the base with both hands, licking the tip slowly and sweetly, savoring my taste as she moaned. Her tongue was soft and wet and hot, every lick a torrent of pleasure.

"This is a beautiful cock, Daddy," she said with a grin, kissing the tip and sliding down. Her tongue lovingly lapped my balls, each stroke passionate and hungry. I could feel her moan as she buried her face, worshiping my cock like it had never been before. Veronica traced the veins with her tongue, her hand gently twisting and stroking my juices out as she slurped dutifully. I moaned loudly, letting go of all but the feeling of her giving mouth. Nothing could compare to the pleasure she gave me, licking and sucking me with so much vigor and passion.

Climax was nearing, my knees locking and my body growing taut. Veronica moaned with my cock in her mouth, picking up her speed as she took me all the way down her soft throat. "I'm going to cum," I moaned, my pleasure nearing with violent velocity. She pulled my dick out of her mouth, kissing the tip as she said, "Good. Give it all to me, Daddy. I don't want to waste a drop." I moaned as she went back to blowing me, her massaging tongue bringing the orgasm to a head.

I gushed deep down her throat as I moaned loudly, her loving motions never stopping. The vibrations of Veronica moaning with me brought forth spurt after spurt of cum. She was cumming with me, her mouth eager to suck all of my seed down. I was her dessert, and she lapped me up like a good girl. Despite myself, my legs twitched as she kept licking and sucking me. My cock was flush and shiny with her spit, being lavished with love.

Veronica looked back into my eyes, and said, "Your turn," before gently releasing my dick. My head was foggy with lust, but I was prepared to do everything she needed. She straddled my chest, her juicy brown ass in my face. With a horny giggle, she thrust her smooth and dripping pussy into my eager and ravenous mouth. I lovingly lapped the lips, running my tongue along her cleft as hot breath escaped. She was sweeter than anything I'd tasted before. I savored her little vibrations and gasps as I licked, my tongue probing to her clit.

"Yeah, Daddy. Suck it slow for me," she gently commanded, wiggling her ass in my face as I feasted better than a king. Her pussy tasted amazing, her smell clean. I pursed my lips around her clit gently, sucking as my tongue flicked against the tip methodically. Veronica moaned, arching her back as she soaked my face in her tasty nectar. Her gorgeous cunt hypnotized me. I buried my face between her ass cheeks hungrily.

Without abandon, Veronica ground against my face, her back arched and moans increasing in volume and tempo. I felt her hips gyrating as orgasm grew near. "Please, Daddy. Please don't stop," she cried, fucking my face with aggressive hip thrusts as she went over the brink. I licked and sucked her madly, catching small breaths as I felt her body tense.

A sweet mouthful of her release was fed to me, and I devoured it gratefully. Veins stood in dense cords upon my limbs as I strained against the restraints. I was dying to grip each cheek, to tear her apart. She was a fire in my core, my primal instincts reawakened in a maelstrom of lust.

Loud, passionate moans echoed throughout the bedroom, her body thrashing sweetly with each wave of ecstasy. Even though I was restrained, I felt in charge, in power. Giving her such sweet release was a gift, and I lovingly licked and kissed her pussy as she rode the orgasm out, wiggling against my face.

Veronica rose, turning to face me. Her dark eyes fogged in lust, a smile upon her face that felt like a trophy to be raised in pride. Every cell in my being was ablaze, my cock hard and crying out for round two. She crawled across the bed, her skin just close enough to smell but too far to taste or touch as she released the restraints on my feet.

She walked near the head of the bed, and leaned over, her face close to mine. "How badly do you need me, Daddy?" she whispered, her cool breath tingling my skin. "So badly. I need you more than I've ever needed anything," I said through lust-clenched teeth. "Good," she cooed as she let my first hand free.

Against all my urges, I patiently waited as she loosened my other hand. Once I was free, I threw her across the bed. She giggled, watching me with rapid breaths, her legs spread for me so generously. I was on her before she could blink, our lips locked as my hands ran the hills and valleys of her curves adoringly. I lifted her feet atop my shoulders, locking eyes as I slapped my hard dick on her soaked pussy. The sounds were gorgeously filthy, and I couldn't wait a moment longer.

Veronica's eyes rolled back as I slowly slid inside of her, inch-by-inch. I relished how ready for me she was, how tight and amazing it felt. As she moaned, I pumped slow and steady, my in-thrust growing larger as I felt her juices covering my balls and the sheets beneath us. I needed her closer, putting her feet down and rolling to my back as I lifted her on top, an asscheek gripped in each hand.

"Fuck, Daddy. That dick's so fucking good," she moaned as I pumped her, listening to the tasty sounds of her pussy clenching me. She was so soft, so warm, so wet—paradise made flesh. I pummeled her, kissing her as we moaned into one another's mouths, our rhythms syncing. My hips were soaked as she gushed cum all around my dick, her eyes rolled back.

"Fuck, baby, you're gonna make me cum," I whispered into her ear. "Cum for me, Daddy. I want you to. You earned it," she whispered before shoving her tongue into my mouth. I slapped her ass, letting it jiggle before clenching again, my balls slapping as I went as deep as I could. I felt her cervical wall, her love tightening around me as we came towards our big finale.

It was an atomic bomb, riptides of euphoria. We came as one, our souls entwining as our toes curled, the bed soaked beneath us. For what must have been hours, we stayed as one, our lips locked and hands pulling one another tighter. After a hot shower, we sprawled back upon the bed. I slept deeper with her in my arms than I had in a long time.

Chapter XIV: The Rattler

Stuart closed up shop at Better Off Read, locking the front door after activating the alarm system. It was growing cool outside, the breeze biting in the darkness. He closed every night, which was fine. It left him a good excuse for stalking the streets. Not that police were an issue, anyway.

He got into his blacked-out hover car, igniting the thrusters as he stared vacantly forward, his tongue running back and forth over dagger-sharp teeth. The taste of blood snapped him out of his stupor, a rich and delicious iron. Life fuel. It had been weeks since he'd killed last, and the urges were growing again—hellish wailing from the abattoir of his black psyche.

Once the craft had fully warmed up, he sped off into the darkness. Anyone would do, at this point. A prostitute tasted quite gamey, although there was always the chance that they had good skin. In the end, it didn't matter to Stuart who he chose, as long as they died screaming while staring into his void-struck eyes. A soul severing its mortal coil was heroin for him—The Rattler.

In a moment of serendipity, a large-bodied prostitute appeared ahead on the sidewalk, her hip cocked and face ready for business. He slowed to a stationary hover, rolling the passenger window down with a quick button press. The large, black-haired woman walked forwards and asked, "Hey, baby. Whatchu need?" "I need a lay for the night. I can pay up front."

"That's gonna be $20,000. You *sure* you need an entire night? I can make you cum faster than you'd believe," she said with a slutty wink. "Oh, I need the whole night. If that's a problem, I can look elsewhere." "No, no, it's no problem. Let me see the money, first, though. I hope you understand."

Stuart understood. He showed his account balance on his transfer fob, to which she nodded. The hooker slid into the car, and after transferring the money, they pulled away. He didn't speak to her as they rode, only drove robotically as his black eyes stared forwards. The Rattler's mind was reptilian—a carnivore, an apex predator, unhindered by petty things like *emotions* or *remorse*. Remorse implied that his victims were equal to him—a truly repugnant notion.

The pair arrived at his little rental house, far beyond the outskirts of Vurisberg. "You live out here, out here, huh?" the whore asked timidly, attempting to laugh. Her fear now was but a precursor. "Yeah, I like my privacy. It's nice to let your hair down, now and then," he said emotionlessly. "I *heard* that! Let's get inside, baby. It's freezing out here."

He fumbled with his key-ring, making his eyebrows knit thoughtfully. "Shit, I forgot to get the front door key copy earlier, before the store closed," he said. "I have a basement entry. It's better than staying out here, though, right?" "Yeah, I don't care *how* we get in," she agreed, shivering and drawing close to him. She smelled of candy—like a cheap floozy.

Everything was in character.

Stuart unlocked the basement door, letting her walk down the stairs in front of him. She went slowly, the steps slick with frost. When they reached the bottom of the stairs, he flicked a switch on the right wall, lighting the basement up. The whore screamed, clutching her face. Her eyes bulged, veins popping on her temples.

Every inch of the walls was covered in human skin stitched together. Cages of swarming insects lined the space—centipedes, roaches, spiders. A massive chair constructed of roughly welded iron sat at the center of the room, a surgical slab set behind it. "Take your seat," he said, his black eyes upon her. In his dominion, there was no cause to play coy.

"Fuck n-n-no. Please, just let me go. I won't say anythi-" she stammered before he sprung forth, his speed and strength completely unnatural. His skeletal hands silenced the woman's yelping, clutching her throat. Stuart controlled her movement through raw force, head-butting her once he aligned her bulky form with the chair. She fell backwards, and once she was in place, The Rattler quickly bound her head, hands, and feet with expert precision.

"Which of my friends wants to come out and play tonight?" he asked of his insect horde, a mad grin upon his face. The spiders were always eager, even if they often went in the wrong direction. However, there was a preference that always seemed to win. A calling card, if you will. The Rattler grabbed a scalpel and a fistful of centipedes from a cage. They writhed, their pointy limbs pricking his hand. He didn't mind, they'd hurt his kill *much* worse.

He sliced huge gouges along the woman's thighs, her breasts, and her upper arms. She awoke, screaming in pain. The sound was music, a dinner bell. With a little prodding, he slid a centipede into the skin of her thigh, where it began to venture and explore its new bloody realm. The outline of its crawling form began bubbling the skin off of muscle in its path. Blood pooled from the deep cut, the insect's motions squelching wetly as it burrowed further under her dermis.

The Rattler continued putting centipedes into her wounds as she wailed; her face red and vocal cords raw. The skin had become loosened quickly; the centipedes exploring her vibrating form with vigor. "They're very good boys," he hissed to his victim. "You're a sick fuck! Why!?" she spat. They really were all the same—humans. He never considered himself afflicted with the condition.

It was really quite sad, going about your life at the whims of those around you. Why bow your head to false prophets, when you could be the King? No matter, she'd not understand his answer. Stuart wasn't sure he *had* an answer for his ways—they simply *were*.

Once the skin had ballooned enough, The Rattler stepped forwards, jamming the scalpel through the woman's eye unceremoniously. She died instantly, blood and the jelly-like filling of her eye oozing down her cheek. He cut circles around her neck, arms, legs, then began carefully peeling the skin. It was best to keep the flesh in one piece, and this technique had taken years of trial and error. Blood had made the floor tacky—a feeling he *loved*, if someone like him could love *anything*, that is.

After an hour of diligent work, Stuart had a wonderful addition to his collection. The centipedes had burrowed into muscle tissue beneath the skin. Their hardened bodies gleaming in blood. "You've done well," he told them, gathering them and returning them to their cage.

With a contented sigh, The Rattler lifted his electric carving knife, and began slicing all the good meat from the skinned corpse. An hour later, he had over forty vacuum-sealed bags topped off with fresh meat. Once the skin cured, he'd stitch it to the walls of the living room. Every day, his temple to murder grew closer to completion. Despite the thrill of the kill, something still felt missing.

It had been far too long since he had stalked prey without it involving a financial transaction. He needed to know his next kill. It had to be that way. Only then, would the soul leaving their bodies *truly* fulfill him. There were so many good choices, but one seemed better than the others. As he tossed the bags of meat into the rusty deep freezer, his next mark came like a bolt from the blue.

She was perfect. From his record pulls, she didn't have any family living in the state. Her job was a revolving door. And better yet, he saw her every day. Veronica. Such a pretty name. She would be The Rattler's, whether or not she knew it. It was time to feed on better meat.

Chapter XV: Home On the Range

I awoke to the sound of knocking at the bedroom door. Groaning, I checked my watch. It was six in the morning. *Allen. You slept through P.T.* I rose, quickly pulling on my robe from the floor. Looking over my shoulder, I took a small moment to just stare at Veronica. She slept so peacefully, her breathing steady and slow.

I opened the door and saw Allen respectfully waiting. He sweated heavily, his breaths still rapid. "Good morning, Leon," he said with a proud grin. "Good morning," I responded through a croaky morning voice. "Why are you drenched, kid?" I asked, slowly taking notice of his keyed-up energy.

"I *did* it, Leon! I did the run, and all the reps!" Allen exclaimed, pumping his fist in victory. "My fucking man! Are you serious?!" "Mhm. Asy is making breakfast, but he has the footage. Did I do good, Leon?" Unbidden of my consent, a tear bloomed from my eye, rolling my face as I smiled joyously. "You did *so* good, kid. Wash up. I'm proud of you. I'll give the video a look after I wake up a bit more."

Al nodded, making his way towards his bedroom suite. I gently closed and re-locked the door. "Who was that?" Veronica asked sleepily from the bed. "Oh, you'll meet him soon. That's Allen. He's a kid I pulled from a bad situation. I look after him now, as best I can. Asy does a good job helping."

"I *love* him, by the way."

"Yeah?"

"Definitely. He's so sweet and helpful. I can tell you this: he didn't resist when I went to shower with you instead of by myself. He knows what *you* need, too."

"I spent a lot of time on his parameters," I said with a low chuckle. She held her arms up from where she lay, outstretching them towards me, beckoning me. Who was I to say no? I dropped my robe on the way to her.

* * *

By the time Veronica and I had gotten dressed, breakfast laid out on the table for us. It was a magnificent spread, the second of the morning. Bacon, eggs, toast, hash browns, biscuits and gravy—we had it all. I made Veronica her plate first, then sat down with mine. After our little morning soiree, we were both starving.

"Hey, Asy," she said from my side as he made his way into the dining room.

"Good morning, Ms. Veronica. Is there anything you'd like added to your breakfast? I have plenty of things I could prepare if need be." She smiled with a piece of bacon in her mouth, shaking her head politely. "No need, I have everything I need," she said with a smile, her hand resting on my thigh beneath the table. "Call upon me if anything you need comes to mind, then," Asimov said, bowing.

How long will it last? How long can anyone hitch their wagon to a delusional, cynical, angry piece of shit like you? Do you really think you're worthy of love?

Leah, a shell put into her head. A toddler holding a teddy bear, its lips blue and bloated. Children, reaching up. Reaching out—to me. Death. Pain.

My face froze in a grimace, my eyes glazed. A hand on my shoulder caused me to jump. It was Veronica. I was home, eating breakfast. Although it was pointless, I held my face in a neutral expression. "Are you okay, Leon?" she asked, her eyes locking with mine.

"I'm fine," I lied. She knew I was lying, but she didn't push the issue. Allen came in to eat after finishing his shower, plopping into his chair and tearing into a heaping plate of eggs. "Hi, I'm Veronica," she said in a cheerful voice, waving her hand at him sweetly. Al looked up, smiled, and said, "Hi, I'm Allen. Are you Leon's girlfriend now, or something?"

A piece of bacon flew from my mouth at the abrupt question. I hacked, while Veronica giggled and patted my back. As I prepared to respond, she cut me off with an answer. "Yes, I'm Leon's girlfriend. You must be his right-hand man." Al nodded, a smile spreading across his face. I beamed like a moron, hastily shoveling more food as I let the two warm up to one another.

"What do you do for fun here, Allen?" she asked. "Leon has a games room. I like to play a lot of shooters there. And last night, I found the library. It hasn't been used in a *while*." Veronica's eyes shifted to me, a playfully judgemental expression on her face. "You have an entire library?" "Yes," I said.

"And you don't use it?" "Haven't in a while." "You're fixing that today," she said with a smirk. I nodded assent, eager to dig into my purchases from Better Off Read, anyway. "I will, indeed. However, something more pressing has come to my attention," I said, looking at Allen.

"Did I do something wrong, Leon?" he asked, his face growing tense for a moment. "No, kid. Not at all. I'm sorry about PT this morning. But you showing the initiative to do it without me showed immense strength and drive. I reward qualities like that. What do you say to firearms training today?"

Al's eyes bugged, and he leaned forward on the edge of his seat. His voice was barely a whisper. "Are—are you serious?" I nodded, and laughed when he let out a triumphant roar, pumping his fists into the air. "YES! HELL YES!" he shouted gleefully. The dining room was a roar of energy and laughter, and we enjoyed the rest of our breakfast.

* * *

"The first thing you need to consider when grabbing or being handed a firearm is safety," I said, my eyes locked intently with Allen. He nodded solemnly, completely focused on my words. "Always check that your weapon is on safe. That'll be the selector, here," I said, showing the switch on the side of the M-16 to him. "After you know it's on safe, you need to ensure that it's cleared. That means that there isn't a round ready to fire in the chamber."

"To do that," I continued, "Lock the charging handle back like this. See that chamber there?" Allen looked where I was pointing, nodding as he analyzed every detail of the gun. "Good, that's where the bullet rests before being fired. No bullet in there means it's cleared and you're ready."

I set the M-16 down on the counter of the firing stall and turned to face Allen. "Here are some rules we *never* break when training or using firearms on operations. Never point the barrel at anyone or anything you don't intend to shoot. Never shoot unless you intend to kill and always check your weapon before and after handling it. Questions?"

Allen didn't have any, so I walked him through clearing, loading, and unloading drills until he was developing muscle memory for it. His motions were measured and confident, and I could tell he was going to be a natural. After letting him run the drills for half an hour, I moved him into the fundamentals of marksmanship. I ran him through breath control, telling him how it's best to fire when at the end of a cycle.

After reviewing sight picture and trigger squeeze, I felt I had adequately covered the fundamentals of firearm use and safety. I'd be close to him the entire time, but I was comfortable that Allen would heed my instructions and use his head. "How comfortable do you feel with shooting some now?" I asked.

"I feel pretty good about it." "Good. I'll be right here. I'm going to activate the pop ups. They'll drop on a successful hit. Good luck, and keep calm." With that, I stepped back and activated the range. Al stood, his face drawn in intense focus, the M-16 at high-ready.

A beep rang out in the range room, and the first target popped up. Allen fired a round and missed. The second shot, however, ripped into the head of the target. I watched intently as it popped down, the next target popping up a moment later. He hit the target at center mass. "Look at this kid," I murmured to myself in amazement.

By the time Al had fired his final round, he had hit nineteen of the twenty targets. I was astonished and knew at that moment that he was born to do this. "Kid, that was amazing. You saw where your sight picture was flawed, adjusted, and executed. You've got this in your blood." Pride shined on his face, adrenaline coursing him from the thrill of shooting. The euphoric tang of gunpowder filled the range, a smell I'd never grow tired of.

"This looks *fun!*," Veronica's voice called from behind us. I turned, smirking at her. "It is. Would you like to try?" I asked. "I do. But not with the rifle. Can I start with something smaller?" "Yeah, no problem. I have a 9 mm here with a fresh clip," I said, turning my attention to her. She walked to the firing cubby besides Allen's, eyeing the pistol, tracing her fingers along the sleek steel.

"Show me how," she said huskily, grabbing my hand and pulling me towards her. I positioned myself behind her, going over the steps I had run Allen through. Her ass wiggled against my crotch as I instructed her, blood rushing to fill my insatiable cock. My instructions became lustily whispered into her ear, and I felt her pushing herself as tightly against me as she could. "Focus, baby," I said, my voice croaking in desire. "You should take your own advice," she whispered back.

By the time Veronica fired the first round, the outline of my dick ground hungrily against her ass. I could feel our heat coalescing. Every cell of my being was crying out to strip her and pin her down over-the-counter right there. Luckily, logic won, reminding me of the adolescent boy less than three feet away from us. A click ensued, the pistol jamming. I stepped back, and when she turned, the barrel was pointed at my chest. "How do I get it to shoot again?" she asked, the pistol barking as it went off.

Chapter XVI: Roadside Buffet

Stuart had the day off from Better Off Read, and boredom was growing. He had paced the dank corridors of his lair for hours, trying to find something to stanch the wailing call of his need to kill. The walls were a tapestry of skins, every color and creed represented. The Rattler was not a picky eater.

With a look at his watch, he knew there might be prey to stalk in the rural back roads. Rednecks and inbreds with nothing to do in the afternoon, no menial labor in walking distance. The taste would be abysmal, but the thrill of the kill stood supreme. The Rattler pulled on a black denim coat, grabbed the keys to his death mobile, and left his lair—a web awaiting to tangle and ensnare.

He slid into the comfort of his black carriage, engaging the thrusters and easing out to coast for fun. The Killing Moon was nearing ascension, his need to slaughter picking up speed at an exponential pace. It was a ravenous beast, claws screeching violently against the steel walls of its captivity. Sparsely dotted rural homes in the distance yielded no prey as he cruised by.

Although his hunger was great, the lapsing hours of futility had Stuart discouraged. Forty miles out from his home, he called an audible, turning his craft right onto an expressway that would loop him back home far more quickly than back roads allowed. His brow furrowed in frustration, the wailing growing all consuming.

Serendipity bequeathed a gift upon the Rattler, thirty miles later. On the shoulder of the road, a family sat by a dead hover van. "Bingo," he hissed to himself, his black eyes consuming them in its gaze. Stuart slowed his craft, pulling towards the side and engaging his four-way flashers. "You folks break down, huh?" he asked hollowly, smiling with his mouth closed. "Y-yes," a middle-aged man answered, putting his hand forwards for a shake.

Stuart shook, nodding sympathetically. "Well, I can give you folks a place to stay until the tow comes. I only live ten miles out." The father mopped sweat off his balding head, his face relieved but apprehensive. With a look back at his wife and the baby in her arms, he nodded. "Yes, thank you. The soonest tow is over five hours out. Come, Marta," he mumbled to his wife, who rose with her suckling babe and climbed into the back of the hover car.

Five miles down the road, Stuart pressed a button on his steering wheel, and the man and woman exclaimed in pain at the same time. Less than a minute later, they were both comatose. Having sedation injectors built into his passenger seats was a decision he'd never regret. The Rattler drove home, his harvest at hand.

* * *

The Rattler never had a live baby before. The prospect of such a delicacy was overwhelming him in pleasure-soaked waves. After dragging their unconscious forms to the basement, he stopped and had a smoke. They were sleeping peacefully, for now. The infant squalled upstairs, where he had left it.

With a grunt of exertion, Stuart tossed the unconscious man into the iron throne of pain, securing him quickly. He strapped the woman down to a surgical slab, then lit another smoke up. The filter impaled upon his sharp teeth as he chewed it absentmindedly. This was to be his entertainment for the next three days, the violent possibilities staggering in his reptilian mind.

Stuart walked upstairs, grabbing the baby up roughly and wedging it under his arm. It squalled and thrashed impotently in his grip as he strolled back to the den of pain. He sat on a steel chair, bouncing the ball of chub on his lap, awaiting the parents' awakening. There was plenty of time, and The Rattler was patient.

It was chubby faced, doe-eyed, and detestable. A light glimmered in the baby's eyes, its pudgy little fingers wrapping around his as he stared vacantly forward. Cooing and smiles fell on deaf ears and blind eyes. He felt nothing for the human race—no genetic coding would save the little one.

"Wakey, wakey," he hissed loudly to the sedated couple. The pair both grumbled, stirring as their eyes opened groggily. "Good. I didn't want to start dinner without the both of you." After another minute, the parents were alert, their groanings replaced by panic-stricken wails and hyperventilating. "You sick fuck! What are you going to do to us?!" the man shouted in the chair, his extremities lined in bulging veins as he battled his restraints.

"I haven't decided yet. Honestly, you two are safe today. I'd be more worried about your precious little spawn here," Stuart said, walking before them with the infant on his hip. "Emile! No! P-p-please. Whatever you want, we will give you!" the father pleaded, while the mother wailed in hysterics. Their eyes locked upon him—just like he wanted.

"I already have what I want."

The Rattler leaned in, his lips pursed against Emile's cheek for a kiss. Just as the baby relaxed, he opened his mouth and bit into the infant's flesh with shark-like teeth. It squalled, shrieking in agony as he yanked his head side-to-side, leaving a gaping hole in its face. The room was alive with the screams of anguish. Blood spilled from the wound, staining the baby's powder blue onesie in maroon splashes.

Inside the cavity, Stuart could see blood and the child's tongue wiggling madly as it shouted. Its face was beet red, wracked in incomprehensible pain. "That's an excellent taste. And you've given me such a pretty meal. Be a shame to not show my appreciation," he said to the man and woman. They screamed, tears flooding their faces as they watched in enraptured terror.

With his free hand, The Rattler unzipped his filthy denim jeans, pulling a sore spotted cock with gray and rippling foreskin free of his fly. Abject dread filled the room—it radiated from the pleading couple. "This should be good. Watch closely and take notes there, Papa." The Rattler locked eyes with the father as he lowered Emile to pelvis height. The baby was half hoarse already from the sheer volume of its cries.

Stuart aligned his festering member with the gaping hole that had once been Emile's cheek and thrust it inside uncer-emoniously. Its frantic tongue spasms were ecstasy against his crusted glans. The cries muffled as he slid into the velvet-soft grip of its throat, thrusting madly as the parents shrieked madly. A few pumps later, and he finished.

"That was a delightful baby. Nice grow-job, Mama. Shame nine months can end this quickly." Stuart let the infant fall to the concrete floor with a small thud, then brought his booted foot down onto its skull. Brain and frayed flesh exploded in every direction from underneath his foot. Emile's cries were then forever more silenced. Blood pooled and flowed to one of the many drains set into the floor.

With a good nut in his system, The Rattler was famished. He knelt, snatching the infant's headless corpse from the floor and walking out of the den of pain. Wordless shrieks and pleas for mercy or death followed him as he left, though he didn't hear a thing. It was suppertime. Man's gotta eat.

Stuart stripped the blood-soaked onesie and diaper from the cadaver, tossing them into a large trash bag. He opened his knife drawer, producing a skinning knife intended for deer. After grabbing a metal pail and positioning it under the dead baby, he brought the blade down the center of its pudgy tummy. Entrails and organs tumbled into the container with a sick, squelching plop. After gutting his meal, he placed the corpse into a large pan with broth, potatoes, carrots, onions, and bell peppers.

The braised baby roast would go for six hours at 325 degrees. He couldn't wait. It was a meal fresher than he'd ever had. The meat would be succulent and tender. As Stuart awaited his meal, he stared into the void, wondering how Veronica would taste as a roast.

Chapter XVII: Take This Job and Shove It

"Leon! Are you okay?!"

I was. Luckily for Veronica, I always wear plates when on the range. My wind had been knocked out of me, but I was fine. "Yeah. Allen, that's what *not* to do. See why I ran you through firearms safety?" I asked with a grimacing smirk. I let out a pained grunt and pulled myself to my feet. Allen nodded, wide-eyed as he stared at me.

"I think I'm done for now. I'm so sorry," Veronica said, frowning and hugging me. "It's okay. Next time, put it down and I'll clear it, okay? These things happen."

Allen was mortified, but calmed as he inspected me. "Are you *sure* you're okay, Leon?" I nodded, patting his back. "I'm fine, kid. We've probably had enough excitement for today, though. You did great. We'll train you more soon." He smiled, nodding and following me as the three of us left the range for the day.

* * *

"Oh my God," Veronica exclaimed as she scrolled on her phone.

I eyed her curiously, asking what was up. Apparently, her favorite author had a book coming out that day. Without a word, I got dressed, awaiting the inevitable question. "Why did you get dressed up?" she asked.

"I assumed you wanted to go grab it. Am I wrong?"

My question was responded to with a gleeful squeal of delight. "Are you serious?! You bought me books yesterday," she said with appreciative awe. I nodded nonchalantly, gesturing around me. "I don't know if you've looked around, but I have more than I need. What's a few books? Especially if it makes you happy."

Veronica torpedoed in for a tight, rib-cracking hug, knocking the wind out of me. She buried her face in my chest, and I couldn't resist running my finger through her silky curls and smelling her. I could stay like that forever—a fact that should have scared me. Something was shifting with every second in her presence.

"You're so good to me, Daddy," she said, her eyes upturned to meet mine. I could see that she was enamored. For once, someone else felt the same thing I did. "You deserve nothing but the best," I said, lifting her face and kissing her slowly. She gently stepped back after, a small wrinkle forming at her brow.

"What's wrong?" I asked. "Freaking have to work this evening. I totally forgot. Got caught up in all of *this*," she said, smiling and gesturing at me. "Why not call in? I'm sure they'll make do." Veronica stopped to ponder, then nodded. She stepped out into the hallway to make her call.

I sat idly on the foot of the bed, letting the peace wash over me. A moment later, I heard shouting.

"Excuse me?! I haven't called out in over a year! I don't think it's fair of you to threaten like this, when *everyone* else gets to call in. Oh? Yeah? Fuck you! I fucking quit! Shove it up your fucking ass, Thomas!"

I tensed as she walked in, but felt relief at her passive expression. "Looks like I'm freed up," she said with a wink. My self control crumbled, and I began cackling at the situation. "What's so funny?" she asked. "I've found someone to match my crazy. Let's go get that book." She smiled, and we made our way to the garage for another impromptu date.

* * *

The Mustang Fiero purred like a kitten as we drove towards Better Off Read. Her hand held mind, thumb tracing the veins atop it. The gunfire and screams were nigh mute to me as we reached Vurisberg proper. Every cell of my body was *present* and devoted to Veronica when she was near. By my count, fourteen murders occurred on the route from Crimson Manor to the bookstore, and I couldn't have cared less.

"I'm so excited!" she said, dancing in her seat as I disengaged the grav thrusters and parked the car. I smiled at her, and we got out and headed inside. Rich incense wafted warmly to us as we stepped through the door. The comfort of subdued red lighting again pulled me into its seductive embrace. Dark instrumental music softly played, the ambience exquisitely gothic.

Veronica hastily made a beeline for the shelf where "Us," by Post-Mortem was. She hugged the paperback to her chest, smiling in appreciation at me. "I'm glad we could get you a copy," I said. "Me, too. Thank you, Daddy." She leaned in, pulling me tightly against her and kissing me deeply. As I smiled at her, feeling her so close to me, a chill washed across my body.

Black eyes feasted upon us from across the room. Stuart, the cashier from the day before, stared ravenously at Veronica, his sharpened teeth glistening in the dim lighting. The sight was unsettling, but I held my composure. Our eyes met then—a primal understanding reached. A killer meets another killer. There was no doubt about it in my mind.

I looked back to Veronica, letting my apprehension abate, if only a little. "Is there anything else you need?" I asked her, and was answered with a happy head-shake. I pulled her tight against my side and felt an icy presence looming. Stuart had crept up to us, practically silent and grinning salaciously at my woman like a feast.

"Can I help you?" I asked, my chest puffing up as he tested my patience. "No, I was just looking for this book. Sorry to intrude," he said hollowly with a voice like a serpent. Stuart reached across to grab a copy of "Us" —and the scent of fresh death met my nostrils. A killer knows a killer, and Stuart had been a very busy boy recently. I held myself between him and Veronica, staring him down until he walked away.

"*That* was fucking creepy," she whispered to me. I nodded, slowly unsnapping the ready straps on my holsters. It never hurts to be ready. After paying for the book, I calmly ushered her out to the hover car and let her in. The moment I made it into the Mustang, I locked the doors and engaged the thrusters. We sped off, my eyes on the rearview as autopilot engaged. Stuart stepped out the door, watching us intently. He was going to become a problem soon. I could feel it.

My thoughts abruptly halted when I felt her hands slowly sliding across my crotch, unzipping my fly. Blood rushed at her touch, my cock engorging and pushing its thick outline against my pants. "Ooooh, Daddy. Look at you, all hard for me," she cooed softly, pulling my dick free. It stood proudly, veiny and flush. Veronica pressed her face into my balls, smelling me, licking me lovingly. Her tongue traced the pulsating blue veins on my manhood, her free hand sliding between my legs and rubbing my asshole.

I lifted my hips invitingly as I slid my pants down, my eyes fiery as I gazed upon her. "You like that, Daddy?" she asked sweetly, kissing the tip with little tongue flicks to catch beads of pre-cum that welled up to her touch. "Mmmhmm," I moaned, spreading my legs for her and clutching a fistful of her hair.

I gently but firmly pushed her face down until her nose touched my pubic mound, pumping the deep velvety grip of her throat. Just as she gagged, I relented, letting her catch her breath. "Now you've got the good spit to do it. Finger Daddy's ass like a good little slut," I commanded in a low voice. She obliged, her finger gently slipping inside of me, arcing deliciously against my prostate as her mouth massaged my aching shaft.

Every lick and motion of her finger was heaven. Before we reached Crimson Manor, I exploded down her throat. Veronica didn't stop sucking until I parked in the garage. She was such a good girl.

Chapter XVIII: Stalking Prey

Veronica's scent still swirled seductively in The Rattler's mind. The man with her could be problematic—it was a meeting of warriors. Troubling. Had Stuart made her his mark sooner, the boyfriend wouldn't be in the way now.

Once their hover car turned out of the lot, he slid into his death mobile and eased out. At first, fear of being spotted kept him a large pace behind. When Veronica's head sank below eye level and didn't resurface, he knew he was clear to follow more closely. Although sex wasn't his motivation, the thought of another man's cock stuffing her mouth made his predatory and territorial urges flare. Blood trickled down his chin in a thick ribbon as he bit his bottom lip.

As expected, the high end craft passed the lower and middle income housing districts, winding northward to where the rich resided. The controlled tree clusters gave way to large sprawling patches, the air a lighter tinge of brown. Physical possessions offered Stuart no comfort, but the resources allotted to those at the top stung, nevertheless. It should be He—the Malevolent King of Warped Flesh—dwelling within a castle upon a hill.

Yet it was not. The Mustang veered right onto a private street that serpentined over rolling hills. He turned, keeping his distance as he saved the path into his watch. It didn't hurt to have this address on hand—there was much surveillance to be done. A few minutes later, his target pulled through controlled gates. The fabled Crimson Manor lay beyond those gates—which meant only one thing: Veronica had shacked up with Leon Crimson.

Unbidden of thought, he felt a primal rage building. Stuart saved the address into his gadget, then proceeded to take photos of the grounds. It could prove useless, but it never hurt to know more. After twenty minutes of diligent analysis, he was satisfied. The Rattler pulled away from the hill, making a mental note of the security cameras dotting the perimeter.

Rage seethed through his gaunt, pale form. The trip home helped soothe his anger. That, and the pair of skins just *begging* to be removed. Emile had been succulent, every strand of muscle tender and juicy. Stuart pushed his speed upwards once Vurisberg limits were behind him.

Mommy and Daddy would undoubtedly be tougher cuts, but he dared not waste the succulent flesh of man. Dilapidated homes blurred by, physical reminders of a rapidly collapsing economy. According to the dash display, the levitating hearse was cruising along at over two hundred miles per hour. The subtle buffeting of the wind against the craft was oddly comforting. Suddenly, blue and red lights flashed behind Stuart, a siren wailing.

Without a peep, he slowed to a halt along the shoulder of

the highway and put the hover car in park. After a moment's wait, a pair of well-armed officers strolled up along either side of the vehicle. The pig on the driver's side lazily rapped on his window with a knuckle, the other hand resting atop his service weapon. The Rattler calmly rolled the window down, grinning.

"Evening, Roy."

"Evening, Stuart," the officer said, extending his open hand. A stack of thousand dollar bills was placed there, the transaction over in seconds. Roy grinned, kneeling to eye level as he spoke in a low voice and pocketed the wad of cash.

"I sure appreciate that. Any favors you need done?"

The wheel was set into motion, then.

"As a matter of fact, officer—I have an address and a name in need of a personal visit."

Weak and raw-throated cries greeted The Rattler's ears upon his return. It was sweet music—a focal point for his rage. Veronica's meat was being defiled by that stumpy blonde cunt. Every drop of cum he shot into her was an affront to his divine pallet. If nothing else, he would keep himself distracted with the pair downstairs until Roy reached back out to him. Having oinkers on the payroll had benefits, even if they rarely presented themselves.

Stuart strolled the walls, running his jagged and dirty finger-nails along the tapestry of human hide. The scratching sound was dry, pleasant. As he walked down the stairwell to the basement, the thrill of impending violence took hold. Hoarse

113

screams continued on, growing in urgency at his presence. The Rattler smiled, watching them with black and hungry eyes.

"Even though you see where I live, you both cry out for help. Who will save you? God?"

He cackled maniacally, strands of gleaming spittle dripping from his fangs. Stuart walked to the wall of cages, eyeing his pets. If he couldn't have Veronica yet, he would make the most of the prey already in his clutches.

"Oh, marvelous. You'll be wonderful for the greasy cunted whore over there," he cooed to a tank of African fire ants. Atop the small glass cube sat a vial, which he pocketed while whistling and strolling over to his table of medical tools.

"Wha-what are you going to do to us? Can't we go? Please?" the husband pleaded, his face red from hours of screaming and crying. Each breath was weak, his voice barely a whisper.

"You can go—on my walls. Your skin is what I desire, though your meat shall not go to waste. I will say this—I'd almost consider keeping you two as breeding stock. Emile was the best meat I've ever had."

Stuart again went into fits of humorless laughter, the father screaming and writhing in impotent rage. The flesh on his wrists completely torn and raw from the rusted iron manacles, coagulated blood blackening the orange metal. The Rattler lifted a speculum from the table, the insertion blades covered in chunks of hardened smegma and dots of dried blood. Mama got the program, wailing atop the surgical slab and flopping like a fish washed ashore.

"Hush, little thing. You haven't even gotten stretched yet," he hissed, walking to the foot of the slab. With a smirk, he ran a fingernail along the bottom of her foot, savoring her helpless squirming. Stuart yanked her elastic jeans down to her ankles, admiring her dark and hairy pussy. Impulse drove him to climb atop her, burying his face in her gash and licking up the flecks of shit and crusted on piss. The stench and sour tang cause his cock to engorge.

"I wonder if you're half as good at pleasing a man as your boy was," he mused aloud between slow and worshipful licks along the cleft of her womanhood. His words met with heartbroken sobs. After one last lick from asshole to pussy, he pulled his cock out, slapping her lips with it as she pleaded for mercy. Mercy would not come, but The Rattler would.

He thrust himself deep inside of her, feeling her hole rip from the dry force applied. Blood and vaginal discharge soaked his crooked and sore-riddled shaft as he pummeled her. Mid-stroke, Stuart noticed Papa wasn't watching. In fact, the daft cunt had the *balls* to close his eyes! Without a word, he pulled his cock free with a wet sucking sound and rose from the table. The Rattler's penis glistened, bobbing as he strolled back to the table. Chunks of hardened vaginal mucus fell in clumps from his dick with each step.

"This should keep you invested in the festivities, Dad," he said coolly. In his hands were a pair of child safe nail clippers. The man was too broken to offer coherent pleas, and Stuart grinned as he straddled him, sitting on his lap. The Rattler pinched Papa's eyelid between his sharp nails, elongating it. A new decibel of scream was reached when he began snipping the eyelid away with the clippers. After two minutes of intentionally slow cutting, the problem was solved.

"There you go!" Stuart jeered flatly. The man's face was soaked in blood, his eyes given no choice but to watch the ensuing pain. With the stage set and a compliant audience, he climbed back atop the bitch and continued fucking her filthy hole. Their cries were a symphony, and he roared as he dumped his load inside of her. The woman wept, and he calmly picked the speculum back up from the foot of the slab, jamming it hatefully inside of her and opening it as wide as it would go. The hole was a tunnel of red flesh, shiny beads of semen dotting her ruined birth canal.

"I know this may come as a surprise to you, but I'm a scientist," he said to the woman while pulling his pants back on and buttoning them. His words fell on deaf ears, but he continued.

"It's true. At one point, I was a highly decorated Entomologist. During those days, I managed to synthesize an attack pheromone for many species of insects. My career ended when I sacrificed our human resources lady to a bunch of jacked up scorpions. But you know what? I'd do it again. That feminist cunt was abysmally annoying, and she never shut up. What I did bettered humanity, if only by a fraction.

"So. I have a wonderful colony of African fire ants in a tank over there. This vial," he continued, pulling the glass tube from his pocket to demonstrate, "contains that pheromone. We're going to see what thousands of ants do to a hostile womb."

It was the same as it ever was—the hostages begged and pleaded and screamed. Stuart uncapped the vial and cautiously administered the pheromone to her vaginal walls. He went to the tank and quickly scooped a cupful of the angry swarm. Mama screamed and pleaded up to the moment he dumped the cup on her twat. The Rattler could feel his pets rage—it was tangible, intoxicating. They bit and crawled and attacked, a sea of red soldiers marching into the freshly bred hole.

Labia blistered and bled, the entrance to her pussy a teeming horde of rage driven insects. Mama convulsed and screamed, and Stuart stood there and enjoyed the show. Blood seeped from her gaping cunt, her screams of anguish no longer sounding human. Papa's unshielded eyes glazed in shock—dull orbs that no longer saw the present, veiled in disassociation. The power in the room was an intoxicant of the highest order.

After his interest waned, The Rattler lifted a scalpel from his table, slicing incisions at various points on her flesh. She didn't notice; the anguish roiling inside of her an all-consuming maelstrom. Stuart smiled at his centipede babies, scooping up two fistfuls. Mama barely resisted when the insects were forcefully shoved underneath her epidermis. They burrowed, the skin bubbling and pulling away from muscle. The walls were going to be that much more complete. Veronica could wait. This was fun.

Chapter XIX: A Gentleman Caller

Veronica and I lounged in the main living room that evening. She paged dutifully through "Talia". After taking notice of her place, I felt impressed at her sheer speed. I read "All the Rage" at a comfortable pace, her head on my thigh. My free hand ran through her silky curls, nothing but the sound of skin on paper in the large room.

I jumped when the doorbell rang. It had been so long since anyone other than Veronica had come to visit. The sound was almost alien to my ears.

"I've got it, Master Leon," Asimov said as he walked by. My curiosity kept me from focusing properly on the book. I marked my place and set it on the coffee table, listening intently. Although I couldn't make out the exchange, I knew it was important when a message dinged on my watch from Asimov. I read it, rising from the couch and smiling at Veronica as I walked away. She grabbed an asscheek and squeezed as I departed, bringing a rush of blood to my dick.

Of all the possibilities, I would never have expected a police officer at my doorstep. The pig was armored from head to toe, his eyes concealed behind a dark visor on his helmet. My mind reeled at what his presence could mean, but I maintained my composure. Appearances are often more important than the truth with law enforcement.

Asy stepped aside politely, remaining by my side as I addressed my gentleman caller.

"Yes, officer? How may I help you?" I asked, my eyes upon the exposed portion of his face. I scanned each motion of his mouth, doing my best to gauge reactions as we spoke.

"Is this Leon Crimson I'm speaking to?" the cop blurted crudely. It was immediately apparent that he had no interest in civility or manners. My chest involuntarily puffed up at his tone.

"Yes. What's this about?" I asked, my voice taking on an edge. Out the corner of my eye, Asimov had engaged his weapon systems. The barrels shined, aching to pump out lead if I gave the word. Without even asking permission, the armored imbecile roughly shouldered his way past me into the house.

"Law or not, you have now breached protocol. Consider your life forfeit," Asimov said, his voice distorting from the power surge of his combat mode activating. I held a hand up to him, stalling the confrontation for a moment.

"Easy, Asy. Pig. You're clearly not here with a warrant. If you were, you'd have started with it. So—what the fuck are you here for? I was enjoying time with my woman," I growled, my fists clenching. The cop's mouth tightened—my instincts told me he was going loud. Before he could draw his service weapon, Asimov fired off a single shot from his arm cannon. The modified round ballooned on impact, blowing the bottom half of the cop's leg off at the knee.

"What's going on?!" Allen cried from his doorway upstairs, his eyes wide in panic.

"Asimov, cauterize that fuck's stump. Get him in the kill room," I said, muscle memory taking over as Spiritcrusher took the reins from Leon. With a regretful sigh, I looked up at Al.

"Everything is okay. This is a crooked cop. Probably on a bad guy's payroll. Are you going to be alright?"

Without skipping a beat, the kid nodded in relief. He went back into his room, gently closing the door. Blood-curdling shrieks soon replaced groggy moans as Asimov seared the stump off with a built-in torch on his arm.

Leah—screaming—forced to eat the flesh of her own leg.

The room spun around me in hateful revolutions, my head foggy and balance thrown. Just as I felt like collapsing to the floor, a hand gently rested on my shoulder. It was Veronica. I was home. Still home.

"Leon—are *you* okay?" she asked, her soulful brown eyes large with concern and sadness. I nodded, catching my breath. Asimov lifted the amputated mouth-breather effortlessly, taking him to a room he'd not leave alive.

"I'm okay. Well—no. I'm not. I promise you I'll tell you about it when I'm ready. It's just—those wounds are still too fresh. I hope you understand," I said, a tear welling in my eye. She said nothing, only nodded and leaned in to kiss me. Her lips were warm velvet on mine, her hand cupping the width of my manhood.

"That's fine. I don't want to make you do anything you don't want to. There's only one thing I want right now," Veronica said, her voice hitching in intensity. My libido ignited with hers. "What do you need, baby girl?" I asked in a low voice, my pulse quickening.

"You're Spiritcrusher. There's a crooked cop in your chamber. A crooked cop who likely has ties to the men you hunt. Crush his spirit—let me watch you do it. Then fuck me," she said, her eyes smoldering embers. I grinned lasciviously, putting my hand on her throat and squeezing just tight enough to make her drool.

"Let me put on my face. I'll meet you downstairs."

* * *

My boots echoed as I walked down the stairs. The feel of freshly pressed fatigues on my skin was like home, my true face in it's throne. There was no Leon. There was pain. Anger. There was only Spiritcrusher. This cunt came to my front door and tried to draw down on me. Whether or not I had an audience, I was going to fucking ruin this man.

Without his black and white armor, the cop was just another run-of-the-mill honky—a pasty, mustachioed bitch. There must have been a police-wide policy for only having haircuts that made you look like a dickhead. The retard had a spiky-topped high and tight, arguably the worst haircut for some-one with three fucking chins. That in and of itself was an accomplishment—one likely attributed to donuts and hours cooping instead of stopping robberies and murders.

Officer Dick-breath jiggled and whined in the torture chair, his hairy chest slick with sweat. Veronica sat naked atop the torture table, rubbing her pussy in slow circles as she gazed upon me. It was gasoline atop a bonfire—my bloodlust rampant and cock so hard it felt like it would burst. I stared at her dark, dexterous fingers as they rubbed a clit shining in plentiful juices.

Focus. Give her something to yearn for.

"So. You clearly were sent here on an order. Whose?" I asked the bound piggy coolly. The fuck-stain spat on me, his logie sticking to my mask with a wet splattering sound. I nodded, completely numb to the pointless defiance that all torture sessions begin with. My gloved hand wiped the phlegm away and slung it to the concrete floor.

"Yeah, you're a real tough guy. Let's see how long that lasts, cupcake," I said with a manic grin. My lovely arsenal of tools beckoned me—a moth to flame. The Daemon had slipped across the veil. All bets were off.

My choices varied and deliciously sinister in their purposes. Blades, files, bludgeons, surgical tools, hardware—I had anything I could ask for. The question of where to start was on my mind, my eyes pouring over the table. While I wanted to hurt him, a strategy was imperative. Starting with a blow to the head could cause unreliable answers. Luckily, there was another head he didn't need.

Veronica sat with her legs splayed, her eyes upon my mask as she slipped two fingers inside of herself and began arcing them slowly, her breasts jumping from her pants and sighs. I smiled behind the mask, grabbing a five-pound meat hammer.

"I ain't fuckin' telling you shit, you vigilante pussy! You can go ahead and just kill me," the cop shouted to me. The hilarity of his crumbling facade was simply too much to bear. I roared mocking laughter, stepping before him and grabbing his stumpy cock firmly.

"You're so tough—a real hard case," I hissed, stroking him until his dick was pink and flush. It was fluffed and ready to go.

"Fucking stop that, you sick faggot! Get your cocksucking hands off my hang down!" he shrieked, his jowls quivering as his face went beet red. Although he protested, his member was very much on board with the treatment it was receiving. I tickled his balls as a final moment of spite, then brought the meat hammer down as hard as I could onto his penis and testicles with a thunderous splat.

Flesh flattened on impact, blood erupting from his puny dick like a fruit gusher being stomped on. His balls exploded into pink mush, the consistency of his former cum storers akin to potted beef. It looked like I had taken a steamroller to his genitals; the skin flattened with burst veins oozing. The floor beneath the chair was soaked in blood as he screamed and rocked in his seat, his head whipping side-to-side as he processed the extreme pain.

Across the room, I heard my girl orgasming fiercely. Her palm made smacking sounds off her pussy as she pumped it deep, moaning louder than the man with a ruined dick. Veronica's eyes flitted from the carnage to my mask as she pleasured herself. I kneeled before the squalling little bacon bitch, savoring his screams a while before continuing my interrogation.

"Okay—oh, shit. I never asked your fucking name!" I barked, laughter bubbling in my throat. His screams slowly died down, eyes glaring into mine. My mirth dried up quickly at his refusal to respond. I reached slowly for his mangled meat, which jolted the fuck back to reality.

"Fuck, please don't. Roy. My fucking name is Roy," he said,

123

his man tits hitching and bobbing as he cried like the pathetic little pussy he was. My cock had never been *this* hard before. I stopped my hand, nodding in satisfaction at his new tone. It was much more submissive—having your dick and balls ruined does that to people.

"Roy. Good name for a douchebag. So, Roy—who the fuck sent you? They couldn't have known who I was, seeing as they sent one retard to do an entire army's job," I said, my hands resting on my hips.

Crickets.

So be it.

I strolled to where Veronica sat, admiring her slick pussy as she rubbed and spread the lips, flashes of delectable pink showing. Without a moment's hesitation, I grabbed a pair of long nails and walked back to Roy. Now that blood had spilled, my ability to improvise pain was chugging along. I pinched one of his nipples, pulling it so hard that it flattened, then pushed a nail through as he flailed and screamed. After piercing both of his nipples this way, I grabbed a nail in each hand, slowly twisting it and causing red beads of blood to well.

"Roy, tell me who sent you. The patience I've exhibited thus far is out of character. It's about to not exist at all. So—who fucking sent you?" I asked, a growl forming in my throat. His silence sent me over the edge. I twisted the left nail so hard that his nipple ripped off, blood running down his bloated gut. The bit of pink flesh landed on the floor silently, his wails drowning out all other sound.

"Fine, fuck. Please, just stop hurting me," Roy rasped weakly after calming down.

"I'm listening."

"Guy named Stuart. Has me on his payroll. Sent me to rough

you up."

I nodded, needing no further elaboration. A killer knows a killer, and the creepy fuck had a hard on for my girl. Seeing as the cop wasn't a pedophile, I was comfortable with the amount of suffering I'd inflicted.

"I won't torture you anymore," I said, pulling a .45 from my cargo pocket and sending a round into his brain. The gunshot rang out, tinnitus in my ears flaring. Roy slumped, blood and brain seeping from the massive exit wound on the back of his skull. I looked over at Veronica, pulling off my mask and smiling.

"Hand me the chainsaw, baby girl."

* * *

I took that pig apart, the floor a pond of blood. Limbs were strewn randomly across the floor. Veronica crawled to me, her path causing ripples in the glistening fluids. My ingenuity kicked in, and I grabbed the severed fist, beckoning her to spread for me. She did so graciously, her eyes vortexes of dripping lust. Slowly, I eased the hand into her, pumping it back and forth gently, feeling her stretch as she moaned.

"You keep working that pussy. Bend over for me," I said in a low voice. Veronica promptly obeyed, fucking herself with the severed hand on all fours. I watched, enraptured by her dark skin and curves. Instead of spit, I coated my hand in the blood pooled around us, stroking my throbbing member until it gleamed redly under fluorescent lights.

Veronica looked back at me, smirking as she shuddered and soaked the detached fist in her creamy cum. I leaned down, kissing each asscheek before aligning my cock with her smooth little starfish.

"I'm going to fuck you in that tight little ass."

"Good. You're well prepared," she said, wiggling it at me.

"Blood makes the best lube."

She turned out to be right, my thick dick smoothly stretching her tight little hole around me. I fucked her like a feral beast in Roy's blood for hours. Stuart was on my list now, but I didn't care while inside of my girl.

Chapter XX: Back to Business

A week passed by after Roy's ham-fisted attempt to kill me, and things had gone back to the norm. Allen and I conducted PT every morning, shot on the range until noon, then gamed for an hour or so. I spent my evenings reading and fucking like a dog in heat. I grew restless, agitated—and I knew exactly why. While I was having fun, what was Precious Cargo Productions doing?

Did I truly deserve these days full of joy and peace? Every fiber of my being told me I didn't. A hallway of dead children laughed mockingly, the echoes of their extinguished flames a haunting blade embedded in my soul. Although Veronica could clearly tell I wasn't well, she never pressed the issue. For that, I was grateful.

My walls crumbled for her on a Wednesday evening. Allen, Veronica, and I were eating another tasty meal, when disassociation veiled my eyes.

Leah weeping, telling me with hitching breaths she loves me, too. A razor shrapnel shell leaves her headless. Her peace is cold comfort.

It mocks, goads, torments.

When I snapped back to the present, my eyes ran rivers down my cheeks. Veronica's hands gripped my shoulders, clutching me tightly against her. Snot ran down my face, the sorrow of the visuals pervasive and enduring. I couldn't shake away the anguish of what I'd done. The warmth of her chest on my face soothing.

I needed absolution, and my opportunity came as a sweet woman trapped in a cruel world. My vision blurred, and by the time I could see through the prism of tears, Veronica had walked me to the bedroom and sat me down at the foot of the bed. Her voice was sweet, understanding, but firm for her next words.

"Leon, I need to know what's happening to you. I know you don't want to talk about it, but whatever's going on is clearly killing you inside. You may trust no one in this world, but you can always trust *me*. Please tell me, baby. Get that hurt out so it can't destroy you."

I could no longer hold it in. Through sobs and ragged breaths, I recounted the events that took place in Unit 378-6. Every wretched moment poured from my mouth, my throat raw by the end of the retelling. I screamed, my eyes dry and palms bloodied by clenched fists. To my shock, she didn't run away. She only held me until my tears had stopped.

We spoke for hours, and Veronica helped me come to terms with my guilt. There was no cure for the pain I felt, but sharing my dark secret helped. I realized as we spoke I had been bottling and fixating. The Daemon was always me. My subconscious mind knew I needed to confess. To be vulnerable. His taunting voice was no longer taunting in the dark realm of my mind.

Something happened, then. A piece of me I thought long broken stirred. The next words only felt natural. I didn't need to think about it.

"I love you, Veronica."

"I love you, Leon," she said, her eyes welling in sympathetic tears as she grabbed my face and kissed me. We held each other and whispered into the early hours of the morning. I slept deeply with her in my arms.

* * *

Upon awakening the following morning, my sense of purpose burned intensely. Veronica slept soundly beside me, her breathing soft and steady. It was time for action. My darkness would never truly die, but the worst part of me was silent for the first time in a while. There was nothing left to distract me from doing what I was put on this earth to do—slaughter the wicked.

My mind ran through strategies, plotting out my assault. I couldn't execute what I intended to do without aid. Allen was absolutely out of the question, which really only left me one choice—Asimov. I'd never call that choice settling, however. With the upgrades, Asy was likely to surpass me in combat lethality.

I rose from the bed, donning my fatigues and boots. Faint sounds of clinking cookware reached my ears from the kitchen. It was too late for PT, but neither Allen nor I bothered that morning. My breakdown likely saved my life, and it had apparently worn everyone out.

I quietly slipped out of the bedroom, making my way down

the grand staircase. Allen sat at the dining room table, his hair messy and face still puffy with sleep. "Good morning, Leon," he croaked groggily.

"Good morning, kid. Sleep okay?" I asked. Al nodded, rubbing his eyes and stifling a yawn. I sat down across from him, stretching my stiff limbs. Moments later, Asimov appeared through the kitchen door with a large serving platter heaped in scrambled eggs, sausage patties, and buttered toast. His other hand held a large pitcher of freshly squeezed orange juice. Asimov set the food between Allen and myself, bowing his head.

"Breakfast is served, Masters Leon and Allen. Is there anything else either of you may need?" he asked.

"Asimov, I believe today is the day I call upon you for a mission. Given my intel, Vurisberg is home to six PCP Op Centers. By tomorrow evening, I want that number cut down."

"Cut down to what, sir?"

"Zero."

Allen gawked at me, the egg on his fork trembling as his hand remained hovering near his mouth.

"That is a tall order, sir. I shall serve dutifully, as always. What can I do to assist in preparations?" Asimov asked.

"Train Allen up for control room operations. I'll compile all pertinent data on our target locations. This op requires constant aerial over watch, so we're going to have to keep Spiritwing airborne. There won't be any room for error. Even with comm jamming, it'll be pretty damn difficult to conceal buildings being demolished. Shoot for a seven o'clock departure. Get to it, Asy. Time to see what those improvements are capable of."

"At once, sir," he said, bowing and leaving us to our breakfast.

Allen's face was still awestruck, almost missing his mouth with the bite he'd been nursing. I chuckled, analyzing the young man's comical reaction.

"What's got you so dumbfounded, kid?"

"Six. Did you say six?"

"Yes, that's the number of buildings in city."

"And you want there to be zero of them—"

"Mhm," I said, taking a heaping bite as my interrogation continued.

"By *tomorrow?!* How can you do that, even with Asy? I'm not saying you can't do it, but—*how* are you going to do it?" he asked, flabbergasted. There was more to his questioning than plan searching. The kid was afraid.

"Kid, I've got gadgets that can level buildings. With Asimov providing fire support, it'll be mostly clearing the first floor and planting explosives, then ex filtrating. Once we're a safe distance, I simply detonate them. I know it sounds like I'm demanding the impossible, but I'd never put myself into a losing fight willingly. You trust me, right?"

Allen nodded, his tense expression softening.

"Good. As far as the control room—your priority is monitoring enemy positions. If they get a flank on us, call it out. You're an incredibly smart kid, and you think quickly on your feet. Breathe, focus on the moment, and you'll do great."

I scarfed the rest of my plate down and rose.

"I've got research to do. I'll see you before take-off. You've got this!" I said, waving as I made my way to the office. There was much work to be done. In approximately twenty-four hours, Vurisberg would be rid of PCP's foothold. I had given them too much of a break—a mistake I'd soon rectify.

No time like the present.

Shit or get off the pot.

Chapter XXI: Immolation of the Damned

The hardest part of leaving for my mission was breaking the news to Veronica. I felt like a monster seeing her expressions shifting at my plan. From an outside perspective, I knew it looked insane. Impossible, improbable, irresponsible—call it what you will. Despite those potent feelings, she spoke in measured words, ever mindful of how they could affect me.

"This is—big, Leon. Huge. Are you *sure* that you and Asimov can pull it off? I don't want to put bad luck on it, but—have you thought this out?"

"I have. Control center's got every scrap of data we could need. Floor layout plans, building occupants, remote control of surveillance equipment. I know it sounds crazy. I do. But if I don't strike hard and fast, it gives them time to bounce back from the strikes I've already laid into them. I can't let all those deaths go unpunished. I hope you can understand," I said, my throat tightening.

"I do. Please be careful. Please."

"I will."

* * *

Dying light surrounded us, Spiritwing lifting off near silently. Asimov sat beside me in the copilot position. Autopilot took us to our pre-programmed designation. I engaged comms.

"Control, this is SC. Do you read me, over?"

"Roger SC, I read you loud and clear. The—uhh—estimated time of arrival is seven fifteen. All weapons systems in 'green status'. Over."

"Thank you, Control. SC, over and out."

Despite the looming slaughter, I couldn't help but beam like a proud father. Asy took notice of my shifting body language, gently patting my shoulder.

"You taught him so well. I can't tell you how grateful I am for that, Asimov."

"The credit is not mine to take, sir. He is a brilliant young man. I foresee him doing great things like you."

"Honestly—I see him becoming *better* than me. Mark my words."

"I shall, sir."

In the distance, our first target came into view—Unit 308-1. Spiritwings stealth systems masked the noise of the rotors, its exterior camouflaged. The craft halted roughly two blocks out from the mark. We each donned our rapid-descent belts to mounting brackets near the doors. In sync, we jumped, the system allowing us to reach the ground in a manner of seconds. With a quick button press, the system retracted quickly, and we were mobile and weapons-free.

I held my Kriss-Vector at high-ready, crouch running from cover to cover. Despite his durable construction, Asimov was near silent in his motions. We moved as one, ghosts on the prowl in the growing darkness.

"SC, Two hostiles guarding the main entrance. Firing distance reads one hundred meters. Over."

I took cover behind an overflowing dumpster, our building a block away. Asimov stood on the other end, guarding the left flank and scanning for contacts. If someone tried to jump on us, they'd fall to bloody and tattered pieces. The thought caused my cock to harden. I cast the distraction aside, focusing on the mission.

"Roger that, Control. Going loud. Over and out." I replied, switching my SMG to 'fire'. My trusty AA-12 was slung over my back. All told, I was carrying easily one hundred pounds of ammunition. Getting rid of humanity's cancer isn't an easy job—but it's worth every ounce of pain. I looked at Asimov, keeping my voice low.

"Asy. Keep your silhouette low, follow my lead. I shoot right, you shoot left when I countdown from three."

"Affirmative, sir. Wilco," he replied, his vocal patterns shifting with his tactical mode engaged. His 'voice' was muffled, quiet. I nodded, and we resumed our advance. At about eighty meters, we reached an adequate firing position. For probably the first time in human history, a mound of garbage served a good cause. Southside garbage men came once a month, and that's only if they felt like it that month. Half the time, they didn't.

I sighted my red dot on my target, aiming at his upper chest.
"Three. Two. One."

The men posted out front of Unit 308-1 collapsed into a bloody heap, their chests hollowed out from the rapid burst of high grade death we supplied. I sprinted forward, keeping myself small on my way to the door. Asimov was right behind me, weapons ready to scream their Hell-forged song. I kicked the door open, weapon raised. Engagement rules were simple: if it breathed, shoot on sight.

Rapid fire bursts rang out, our clearing of the floor a coordinated genocide that beautified the sea of unwashed faces. The floors were tacky with blood, shell casings and decimated corpses clogging the concrete hallways. Our detonation point was at the center of the floor, where the elevators were located. Before we rounded the corner, I halted.

"SC, I have ID chip readings on five hostiles at your detonation point. Proceed with caution."

The healed bullet wound on my arm was a reminder to not round corners blind. Halting, I pulled a rapid detonation grenade from my ammo vest. I calculated the ideal trajectory for a toss, pulled the pin, and sent the steel orb of doom around the corner. The scumbags only had about a second to scream before the explosion obliterated them. Blood hit the wall opposite of Asimov and I, chunks of innards splatting and sliding down slowly. Smoke and the scent of cooked human flesh filled the space with a stench that made my mouth water and my stomach buck sickly.

Asimov and I rapidly rose and entered the clearing. Viscera and disparate limbs soaked the filthy floor. Sadly, there was little time to admire our handiwork. I pulled a cylindrical sleeve of bugs from my vest, dumping them out. They scurried away to optimal blast positions. It was time to go. We charged the hallway towards the back entrance, laying bullets into a few dozen wastes of life en route to our exfiltration point.

I kicked the door off of its hinges on the way out. Asimov and I simultaneously activated our rapid-descent belts, tossing the leads upwards. A pair of metallic pings greeted my ears, the systems attached to the mounting brackets. We pressed the button on the belt again and rocketed through the air. I quickly unclipped, taking my place in the pilot seat.

Spiritwing gained altitude, veering south towards our next target. A mile out, I activated the drones, enjoying the show. Unit 308-1 became an infernal pillar of flame. It crumbled, the entire structure reduced to a mound of rubble. One down, five to go. I was having a damn good time, but it was going to be a very long night. We flew onwards—there were still plenty of pedophiles left to kill.

Chapter XXII: The Hornet's Nest Swarms

Units 302-9 and 303-4 went down much like our first target. With three locations down, I tallied our kill count to be over six thousand. It was a good day for fans of violence, my pants sticking to my legs where oozing pre-cum had dried. All this violence was a rush—a high unlike any I'd experienced before. Pedo genocide, gotta love it!

We were nearing midnight, the streets beneath us swarming in riots and confusion from the impromptu demolitions. Vurisberg was a swarming hornet's nest—a throng of bloodthirsty beasts uncaged.

"Looks like we have to infiltrate from the roof for the last three, Control. Recalibrate Spiritwing's course, over."

"Roger, Wilco, SC. Over."

I let out a sigh, knowing how much harder things were about to get. We had been breaching on ground level, because that was the path of least resistance. A topside detonation would likely involve more combatants. It was a lose-lose situation, but I wasn't letting it diminish the fire raging inside me. A roof side drop-off beat rolling through a sea of disenfranchised and berserking people.

Unit 312-02 came into view, and I burst out into brays of laughter. Asimov looked me up and down a moment, before asking, "What's so funny, sir? I fear my emotional context parameters are malfunctioning." I shook my head, pointing below us. They had placed every guard on site at the bottom entrance.

"Looks like we won't have much to worry about going topside on this one, Asy. I don't know how long it will hold, but we just got lucky. They must have heard we were breaching on the ground floor. Fast and hot on this one. Be ready," I said, inserting a fresh magazine and chambering a round.

"Ready to execute with extreme prejudice, sir," Asimov said, his barrels gleaming and ready to spit hot lead. I nodded, Spiritwing coming to a stationary hover over Unit 312-02's roof. We connected our descent rigs, jumping down to the helipad below. Our feet made light contact, we disengaged our belts, and headed to the roof entrance.

The roars of the teeming masses far below drowned our footfalls out. I tried the door and found it locked.

"Asy, crack this lock," I commanded in a low voice. Regardless of the surrounding chaos, losing tactical awareness and the advantage of stealth was something I'd not do. He nodded, the metallic rings on his index finger retracting to reveal a slim multi-tool. Within a few minutes, he was done, the door slowly opening of its own accord.

I took point, sweeping the stairwell with my Vector. Our descent was slow and methodical, and I halted just outside the door. I pressed a button on my earpiece, keeping my voice low.

"SC, Control here."

"Control, SC requesting a full building thermal scan. Ping all contacts to my watch, over."

"Roger, SC. Wilco, over and out."

Not thirty seconds later, my watch lit up. I grinned beneath my mask. The top floor was completely vacant. They clearly had moved everyone down to the lower floors. I motioned at Asimov, and we quickly went through the doorway. The corridors were wider on the top floor, the walls less filthy, the floors not covered in bodily fluids and discarded syringes. Soon, every floor would be equal—burnt to cinders and rubble.

I took the lead, walking with purpose and speed towards the elevators. It was eerie, strangely quiet around us. Asimov took guard while I produced another sleeve of bugs and poured them out. We rose, sprinting back to the stairwell with our weapons at high-ready. As expected, we met no resistance on the way back out. This was it—the calm before the storm.

Who knew how PCP would adapt after this strike? Given the rapid disappearances of four locations, I knew they couldn't be thrilled. The thought made my loins stir, the millionth libido surge of that blood-soaked night. Once we were back topside, Asimov and I engaged our belts, tossing the leads upwards and ascending back to our craft.

Spiritwing engaged, carrying us away from Unit 312-02. A mile out, I detonated the bugs. The fire show was beautiful—damned souls trapped in a whirling conflagration. Whether or not there's a God, I could give them the Hell they deserved, if only for a little while. Eight thousand scumbags down, the world to go. Let the wicked suffer.

Unit 323-99 was less than ten miles out, the night sky lit

up by all the riots and explosions. So far, I had found PCP's tactical readiness wanting. I suppose when you've got everyone in your pocket; you don't expect vengeance to come knocking at your door. Their complacency was my advantage. I looked below us, noting the unfolding mayhem.

Rioters and PCP guards were engaged, batons lashing out and rocks flying.

"Control, halt here for a moment. We have civilians engaging PCP forces. I want to see how this plays out, over."

"Roger, SC. Route plan has been paused, over."

"Come on, Asy. Watch the show," I said, gesturing to the impending violence.

From my vantage point, it was apparent that de-escalation wasn't a skill taught to PCP grunts. They laid into the rioting swarm, batons crunching eye sockets and smashing noses into bloody pulps. The power was shifting, however—an expertly aimed stone took a guard smooth out, embedding into his face. As he fell, it was like the floodgates had opened. Vurisberg citizens overwhelmed the PCP soldiers, punching, kicking, biting.

The people below did not stop at the guards. They roared into the building, their bloodlust not sated. I could relate. Show was over, and the result was another blessing in a night full of carnage.

"Control, resume scheduled route, over."

"Roger, SC, resumed. Over."

I couldn't have asked for a better development. With PCP forces tending to the rioters on the lower floors, I could make a quick bug deposit and be on my way to the final ops center in the city. Spiritwing halted, hovering over the rooftop, where we descended and made our way down the stairwell after cracking the lock. I pinged my watch, initiating a floor-wide heat signature reading. There were two signatures on the floor, both in an office.

Despite my adrenaline, I knew this could give me more potential leads.

"Control, SC here. I need you to feed me audio from the top brass having a chat, over."

"Roger, SC. Patching the feed to you now, over."

The audio crackled for a moment, sharpening with Allen's tweaks from the control room. The voices were both male. I listened intently, taking a knee just beside the door.

"Four locations, George. Four fucking locations."

"I know," George responded exasperatedly.

"In ONE night. Whoever is doing this has resources and experience. I wouldn't be surprised if they came after this building in the next few days."

"Well, what do you propose we do about it, aside from bolstering our security?" George asked. A silence passed between the two men for a moment.

"The Rattler."

"The Rattler? Are you *certain* it's a good idea to call upon him? Don't get me wrong, the guy makes some of the best snuff I've ever seen, but—he has a tendency to go overboard," George said, his voice rising a semitone in fear.

"That may be so, but in *this* situation, I'd say overboard might be called for. Wouldn't you agree?"

The question was met with another pregnant pause.

"Fuck, Lawrence. Let me clear it with Richard Vostares. You know he hates being interrupted when he's on vacation."

"Fuck, who wouldn't be?!" Lawrence said humorously. "I know if I had an island of kiddies to plow, I'd want to be left alone, too!"

"Agreed. Hey, Richard. Sorry to disturb you, but—yes. That's right. Seeking clearance to reactivate The Rattler. Oh? Excellent. Thanks. Bye."

"So? What'd he say? Was it too outrageous a suggestion?" Lawrence asked, goading his superior.

"No, surprisingly. The Rattler will be reactivated tomorrow. So, catch that Tampa Bay Lightning game last night?"

"Oh, I wouldn't have missed it—"

I had heard enough, killing the feed. Richard Vostares— something in that name caused a cool chill to run through me. The Rattler raised my hackles, as well, though not to the same extent. It was a strange gut feeling I couldn't shake. With a nod to Asimov, I opened the door and crouch-sprinted towards our mark, my Kriss Vector scanning for movement along the way. As expected, we encountered no one. The rioters below were likely pushing PCP agents' shit in. It always feels good to see someone else do your work for you. Serendipitous, really.

The bugs zipped to their programmed locations, our task complete. I ran back towards our exit, when a voice called out loudly-

"Hey! Who are you?! What are you doing here?!"

I had enough time to lay eyes on the sleazy man in a suit before his face became a crimson hole. His form crumpled, blood spreading beneath as limbs twitched sporadically.

"We've gotta exfil, and fast," I hissed to Asimov, his gun barrels still smoking. Asy nodded, and we ran as fast as we could to the exit door. The stairs clanged underfoot, my adrenaline surging. With the gunshot, it was likely the other man would catch on to our presence, and quickly. We ascended, my lungs aching as Spiritwing made its departure. I looked back at the building, its destruction but a button press away.

Spiritwing hit the mile point, and I blew up building number five of the night. The explosions were gorgeous; the building raining down a hail of concrete chunks. Anyone down there was likely to become a pancake. We made our way to Unit 333-5, the name Richard Vostares echoing through my mind. The last stop of our mission was to be the hardest. We flew on.

Chapter XXIII: One More Hill to Climb

Our luck came to an abrupt and violent end as we neared our final target. It was almost two in the morning, and Unit 333-5 was lit up and swarming with armed guards. The rioters were already engaged with the ground guards, while the roof had twenty gunmen standing by.

"Fuck," I hissed angrily. Asimov watched, patiently awaiting his orders while I concocted a workaround for the new challenges presented. The bottom entrance was out of the question, and the roof looked almost as suicidal an approach. Luckily, I never let a problem stump me for too long. I reached into my vest, fishing out a concussion grenade from an inner pouch.

On most missions, I wouldn't have even brought them. They were proving vital, now. I slowly formulated a plan, eyeing the hostiles and combing over every aspect of our approach. After another moment, it came to me.

"Asy. We're going to have to deal with the cunts on the roof quietly. Hand to hand only, okay? Gunshots would be heard below, and we really can't afford to get detected. This is it. This is the last scrap of PCP in our city, and we can't afford to blow it. Are you ready?" I asked, pulling my clawhammer free in my dominant hand. I'd need one free for disconnecting from the craft.

"Yes, sir. I shall do whatever the mission calls for. It is an honor bringing justice upon these foul men, Master. One I shall never forget." I couldn't have been anymore proud of the team I had. It was a feeling worth dying for, worth killing for. I had one last affair to address before tossing out the grenades.

"Control, SC here. This is going to get hairy, even if we pull everything off perfectly. I want you to know—want you to know how proud I am of you. Just breathe, and you'll do great. We're about to take our city back, kid."

"Roger, SC. I will do everything I can to get you home in one piece. Thank you for letting me get to feel like a hero. Good luck. Control, over and out."

Spiritwing idled over the building, the gunmen below oblivious to our presence. Asimov and I latched our systems, prepared to move with rapid lethality. I pulled the pin and dropped the grenade amongst the crowd. They hardly had time to react before it sent out a blue pulse of kinetic energy, knocking them flat. We dropped amongst them from our hidden vessel above, disconnecting our belts and ready to get to work. Go time.

The man at my feet hardly made a sound when I brought the claw side of my hammer into his eye socket, ripping it free through the side. His body twitched, blood and brain matter seeping out of the new orifice I'd given him. Asy and I went to work, smashing skulls and silencing the opposition in a lightning fast procession.

I brought my baton and hammer down onto heads, into faces as guards struggled to rise to their feet. Within five minutes, nothing but the dead lay at our feet. I nodded grim satisfaction, motioning for Asimov to take point. He tried the door, found it locked, and began splicing the security system. If he drew fire upon the door opening, it wouldn't kill him—another reason for handing him the breach role on our last stop.

I couldn't say why, but a sense of dread washed over me while Asy cracked the door. Our game plan had gone smoothly so far, but the importance of this ultimate target was all-consuming. The closer I got to wiping PCP out in my city, the more I feared it would all go catastrophically wrong. The Rattler—a name I'd heard amongst snuff circles. Richard Vostares—a name all too familiar. My mind reeled, searching for an answer.

"Master, the door is breached," Asimov said, snapping me from my daze. I nodded, following him down the stairwell. My SMG had two mags remaining, the AA-12 on my back aching to play. Before allowing him to breach the door to the main floor, I pinged for heat signatures. My jaw dropped—there were easily fifty men between me and my destination.

"Control, SC here. I'm picking up a lot of signatures here. How many weapons systems can you detect? Over."

"Fifty-two systems, SC. Over."

"Fuck. Okay. Asy—guns blazing looks like our best choice. If it goes sideways—mission comes first. Do you understand?" I asked, my voice firm on the last remark. He looked me up and down for a moment, then nodded. With that, I motioned for him to proceed. One more hill—I just had one more hill to climb. I only hoped I could make it there, my trigger finger itching. Death never scared me—only failure.

The door clicked, ready to be kicked open. Asy looked back at me, receiving a go-ahead nod in confirmation. His kick took the door off its hinges, flying thirty feet and splattering a man standing on the other side. Blood seeped around the hunk of dented metal embedded in the wall. I made a mental note—fifty one to go. There wasn't time to think, small arms fire screaming out as Asimov entered the corridor. The rounds plinked off of him impotently, flattening against the breastplate of his frame and falling to the floor. He returned fire, barrels rotating and flaring while he unloaded.

My cock again stiffened, the anguished wails of Asy's victims a beautiful symphony. I burst through the doorway, taking cover behind him and sighting in on the distracted targets. Heads burst from my deadly aim, the kill count ticking upwards at a steady pace. Fifty-one cut down by at least twenty, the adrenaline rush severing time's relativity. That was why I didn't notice the men setting up a rear flank.

"SC, Control here. Hostiles on your six, over!"

I pivoted, firing on the first motion my eyes caught. The shot was low, ripping carotid arteries in a messy gush. More contacts replaced him, my fallen foe bleeding out and weakly gurgling blood like a pathetic little bitch. Two more men fell with their weapons raised, heads popped. Then, my SMG clicked. I had run dry.

My motions were frantic, desperately slinging the AA-12 and racking a shell. Multiple rounds hit my plates, and judging by the faint sting—I had been shot through my plates. My trusty automatic shotgun chanted its deathly bark.

DUNDUNDUNDUNDUNDUNDUN!

Heads and limbs severed, the razor shrapnel shells tearing

my targets asunder. I lost count of how many rounds I'd fired before the last hostile lay slain, blood pooling on the filthy concrete floor. Innards and hunks of sliced flesh clung to the walls, sliding down slowly and leaving a grisly trail in their wake. I stayed in my kneeling position, the sounds of gunfire now echoing, my ears ringing from a painful sting of tinnitus.

"Sir. Sir! Are you alright?" Asimov asked, shaking me gently. I realized I'd been dissociating for a moment, pain in my side screaming. I'd been hit pretty good, my body slowly growing colder as I bled. I shook my head, pulling out a sleeve of bugs and handing it to him.

"Sir, allow me to put you aboard Spiritwing first, at least."

"No. Mission. Mission comes first," I grunted through pain-clenched teeth. Asy offered no more arguments, nodding and striding away quickly with the explosives. Things blurred around the edges, pain growing and sweat pouring profusely. In those moments, I felt as though death were at my shoulder. Blood soaked my pants where I lay, the floor cool.

My eyes scanned the drab walls, and a photo caught my attention. PCP Headshots, big cheeses peddling child flesh and suffering. The photo I'd focused on was none other than Richard Vostares, CEO. His face stared back at me—the man who raped me. The man who caused the broken Leon I'd become. I grew colder still, hoping Asy would be able to extract safely, with or without me. All went black.

Chapter XXIV: Delectable Discoveries

Two weeks passed since Stuart had been called upon by Precious Cargo Productions. In that time, Papa met the same fate as tender little Emile and juicy-cunted Mama, and the prime directive from Richard had been made crystal clear—find who was responsible for wiping out the Vurisberg centers. Stuart had feelers out amongst the city, listening and reporting. It was only a matter of time.

With his final hide cured and stitched, the living room was covered completely in skin. From the walls to the reupholstered couch, everything had been lovingly hand sewn. Work was disappointing in those two weeks—Veronica had not come to buy books. It was frustrating beyond belief. He needed to watch her eyes as the light faded more than anything. The hunger was pervasive and all-consuming, dousing his mind in a wanting flame.

The Rattler sat on the couch, his sharp teeth ripping off a chunk from a steaming hunk of meat. Whoever had moved on the PCP locations likely lived in the area. It was probably a group, people with resources and training. No surveillance footage could be salvaged, the feeds hacked before the assailants entered the premises. Richard's men had combed the cloud, pouring over hours upon hours of footage. It was a bust—the feeds were all hacked and replaced by still images.

With a glance at his watch, Stuart rose and prepared for work. The hunger screamed inside, but he paid it no heed. His next kill had to be Veronica. No one else would do. He made his way out the front door, cranking the death mobile and easing out of the driveway.

As he drove into Vurisberg proper, the residual effects from that night were all around. The windows of many shops had shattered and were taped over with cheap plastic sheeting. Everything bore a thick coat of dust, the force of the explosions sending clouds of rubble and crushed concrete throughout the city. There was an undeniable edge to the faces Stuart looked upon while driving, a restlessness and discontent.

Simply put—another riot was inevitable. The Rattler drove on, savoring the delicious violence in the air. It was a feeling unlike any other, knowing how many more lives could end soon. He turned right into the parking lot of Better Off Read, his fingers tapping the wheel absentmindedly.

Scattered daytime whores limped through the morning light, squinting as they headed to whatever rathole motel they lived in. It was nine-twenty in the morning, the time for those of the night to make themselves scarce and recoup for another bout of debauchery. Stuart parked his hover car, watching time tick by. The hunger dwelled in his mind, swirling. It was time to open the shop.

Stuart crossed the lot, entering the security code into a number pad. After a beep, he let himself in and turned all the lights on. Most of Better Off Read's sales came in the evening time, but coffee was a draw for non readers. In this economy, it was paramount to eke out profits wherever they presented themselves. With the automated coffee bar powering up and the register online, his job was essentially done.

The copy of Stuart Bray's "Broken Pieces of June" trilogy he'd been reading beckoned from the shelf behind the counter. It had been a deliciously depraved read so far, and there were eight and a half hours to kill. Dungeon synth played softly over the store's PA, atmospheric and dark. Although the place could do with more skin, it was as comfortable a place as any for The Rattler. A perfect place for someone with so monstrous an appearance to blend right in. He read, seated on a black stool behind the counter, his mouth watering over the violent passages.

Hours dragged by, the odd customer popping by to get caffeine or another book. By one in the afternoon, foot traffic livened up a little. The space became filled with hushed voices of people gushing over books to one another, cooing over covers, enjoying themselves. It was arguably the worst part of the job—people. Fighting the urge to slit their throats with a broken coffee pot was a colossal undertaking. If the hunger wasn't sated soon, Stuart worried he might explode.

To keep himself occupied (and to satisfy the mission he'd been assigned), The Rattler scrolled through documents on his phone. He chased leads, dissecting the data for any clue, no matter how small. The process was tedious, and by four p.m., his head ached and teeth gnashed in frustration. That was when fate dropped a juicy pie into his lap—Veronica's scent drifted to him.

There she was, standing alone at a shelf, grabbing every book she could. Saliva pooled in Stuart's mouth at the sight of her, juicy and delectable. Her bubbly ass ached to be slow cooked, her skin lovingly peeled away. It took all of his control to not leap towards her. He kept his eyes downward, concealing his intentions as she walked up to the counter.

"Good evening," Veronica said in a tired voice, bags beneath her eyes. Her body language was stiff, half-distracted.

"Good evening. Find everything you were looking for?" Stuart asked, masking his frantic need to hurt her. She nodded, awaiting the total. Once he rang up the last item, she swiped a pay fob quickly, grabbing the bags and leaving without a word. That would *not* do. Not at all. Once Veronica had walked out the door, he leaped over the counter and pursued his prey.

Her luscious curls bounced as she walked to her car. The smell of her was maddening, and he couldn't go any longer. Before The Rattler could get close enough to grab her, Veronica turned quickly, a pistol drawn and pointed at his face.

"Back off, you fucking freak. This is *not* the time to be pushing me," she growled, the pistol shaking from her adrenaline. Stuart did his best to play coy in response. "Ma'am, whatever have I done to make you uncomfortable?" he asked, keeping his expression neutral. It didn't work. Clever girl.

"You know you're being a creep. I have a man. A better man than you, by far. I can definitively say he's never stalked me as I shop or followed me to my car for no reason. Back off."

The Rattler could no longer conceal his true face. Veronica's surge of rage was an aphrodisiac.

"He's not a man. A man would keep you locked up so you can't get away. A man would be around to protect you," he hissed, his teeth bared. Those words sent her into a berserk, her face red and eyes narrowed to hateful slits.

"He's never far. For one, he trained me on this pistol. For another, he can be here in seconds if he needs to! You don't scare me!"

"Tell that to your shaking hands. Here in seconds, eh? Must have a small militia on board. How long do you think it'll take me to slit your throat?" The Rattler asked, slowly inching closer to her. It had been a miscalculation on his part—Veronica fired off a round, the bullet grazing his face and carving out a deep groove.

The pain took a while to register, but Stuart halted and stared Veronica eye-to-eye. Blood poured down his jaw from the fresh wound, his teeth dripping slobber as his fists clenched. Veronica took advantage of his pause, throwing the bags into the passenger seat with the pistol still trained forwards.

"I hope your man is strong," he hissed, ready to strike.

"He is. He's fucking Spiritcrusher!" she shouted, firing a round past his head and throwing herself into the car. Before he could grab her, she slammed the door and locked it. Veronica sped off, leaving Stuart reeling. Things all made sense now. He pulled his phone from his pocket and made a call.

"Richard, it's Stuart. I know who blew the ops centers. I also know where they live. Before I tell you that—can you still remotely stall vehicles out? Yeah? Perfect. I'll send the license plate number, now. It's time to get even."

Chapter XXV: Descending

My recovery the past two weeks had been arduous. Even with Asimov's parameters and the full range of medical equipment provided by Crimson Industries, a shot to the kidney fucking sucked. I was up and mobile again, eating breakfast with Allen and Veronica, but my range of motion was still limited from the injuries. It was a miracle I didn't bleed out before Asy got me to the medical bay. For that, I would always be in his debt, machine or not.

Veronica had finally calmed down by the end of the first week over my condition. It took a lot of insisting to convince her I was quite capable of feeding myself. With anyone else, that might have annoyed me. With Veronica, it just made me love her more. The human mind's a strange and silly place, sometimes.

Although the specifics still eluded me, Richard Vostares was a chief priority on my list of targets. I could feel terrible memories hiding in my subconscious, aching to either destroy me or fuel a righteous surge of murderous rage. It wouldn't help torturing myself until I was well enough to do something about it. I took a bite of my parfait, feeling Veronica's watchful gaze.

"Yes, Mama, I'm eating," I said with a smirk. She nodded, gesturing for me to proceed. I chuckled, obliging her. It's hard to be irked by people trying to take care of you, as alien a feeling as it was. We finished our breakfast, Allen going to shoot at the range under Asimov's supervision. Just when I thought I couldn't be more proud of the kid, he proved me wrong. Despite my absence, he continued training hard daily.

Veronica and I lounged in the living room, my head in her lap as I paged through "Consumed by Rage", David Hardy's sequel. My time recuperating had also been one of self-discovery. Reading kept my mind occupied, healed me in ways that were both hard to define but incredibly tangible. Her fingers ran through my hair as she read "Talia" for the third time.

While a normal person would have spent a few months reading all the books I'd purchased for us, Veronica had devoured them all in the first *week* of me being in recovery. I could feel her growing restless with nothing new to read and a man too hurt to go out safely. It made me feel sad for her, guilty.

"Baby girl," I said, my eyes shifting upwards to her.

"Yes, Daddy?" she asked sweetly, placing her book down on the arm of the couch. I grunted, easing myself to an upright position.

"How would you like to get yourself more books? I know you've got to be going crazy with all this downtime."

"I'd like that. Are you sure you don't need me to stay here?" she asked, her hand gently cupping my face. I shook my head, putting on my big boy face so she'd believe me.

"I'll be okay for an hour, love. Just be sure to grab your pistol before you leave, okay? That Stuart guy was bad news, and it doesn't hurt to be too careful." Mention of the Better Off Dead employee caused Veronica to physically recoil and shiver.

"Yeah, I'll have it ready. I'm so grateful, Leon. It's not just how generous you are. It's—it's how much you care. Allen and I both love you so much. I hope you know that."

"I know, baby. I love you both, too. I figured you'd like something to keep yourself entertained until I'm bedroom ready again," I said with a chuckle. Veronica playfully swatted my arm. A devilish look crossed her face afterwards—a look I'd learned quickly. Without another word, I gingerly slid my pants down. She took me into her mouth, giving me everything I needed.

* * *

Veronica had been gone for over an hour, which was concerning. I called her, limping stiffly through the house. After a few rings, she answered, her voice distressed.

"What's wrong?" I asked, my heart racing.

"I fucked up, Leon. I fucked up bad. I'm so sorry."

"Slow down. Easy—what happened? Step by step. Breathe."

She panted for a moment before answering again.

"That fucking Stuart guy. He tried following me to the car, and was threatening me. I shot him. It didn't kill him, just cut his face. Then—then I said who you are." Veronica wept, her sobs hitching and distraught. I knew what she meant, my body flooding in a glacial wave of fear. Even if it was just a creep from a bookstore, loose ends were dangerous in my field of

157

work.

"Fuck. It's—it's okay. Just come home. I'll have Asimov on patrol mode, get Allen kitted up, as well. Where are you?"

"I'm about ten minutes away, Leon. I—FUCK! NO! God fucking DAMN IT!!!" she shrieked in rage. Before I could even ask what was going on, she continued.

"The car just stalled out, Leon. I don't know what happened. All the dashboard lights just turned off and it died. What should I do?" she asked, hyperventilating. Hardened instincts from countless hours in high-stress situations came flowing to me.

"Stay put. I'm coming to you. Allen and Asimov will monitor all the security systems here. Keep your gun out and ready. I love y—"

The call disconnected, loud beeps ringing in my ear. Something was very wrong. I shouted for Asimov, making my way to the armory as quickly as I could. He quickly caught up to me.

"Yes, Master Leon? How may I serve?" Asy asked.

"Switch to defense parameters, and get Allen armed. Veronica's car just got hacked, and my true identity is compromised. Code fucking red," I said, my teeth clenching in pain as I pushed myself to move faster. My gunshot wound stung, an internal pulling that was dull and agonizing.

Asimov left to attend to his orders as I grabbed my AA-12 and two magazines. For one guy, it was certainly overkill, but I had a dread building in my stomach that I couldn't ignore. I limped stiffly to the garage, where I made a beeline to the closest vehicle. After engaging thrusters, I flew from the property on a collision course with what was to become the worst day of my life.

* * *

By the time I reached Veronica's car, it was empty. Her bags of books were on the passenger seat, her pistol on the floorboard. Blood dotted the seat—a clear sign of a struggle. I screamed, thrashing despite my healing wound. She had been so close to home. Things only worsened when my watch pinged with an invitation to a live video feed. The host's name was a blade of doom—The Rattler.

Chapter XXVI: Live Feed From Hell

My earpiece beeped before I had a chance to dial Asimov.

"Master, are you receiving that feed?"

"Yes. Trace it. For the love of everything, trace it," I said frantically, the video grainy and out of focus on my watch. A crude iron chair sat in the center frame, rusted cages behind it full of skittering insects.

"I'm on it, sir. A rough estimation has already been projected to your GPS. We shall defend Crimson Manor. Good luck."

"Good luck to you both. Tell Allen I love him, Asy."

"I will, Master Leon."

Our call ended, my adrenaline pumping furiously. I gingerly slid back into the driver's seat of my craft, setting the GPS to the coordinates sent from Asy. The longer the feed went, the better triangulation would be. Given the data already parsed, my target was outside of city limits. I sped off, enabling autopilot. The video feed filled me with dread, a tightness in my chest.

For several minutes, nothing happened. I stared at the empty iron chair, hoping beyond hope I could reach that red room in time. Then, The Rattler stepped into frame. It was fucking Stuart. He was nude, stroking a diseased looking cock as his hollow eyes stared directly into the camera lens. It felt like he was looking right at me, daring me to make a move.

"Spiritcrusher—you've been a very busy boy lately. Blowing up buildings, putting your cock where it doesn't belong—you've done it *all!*" he hissed, mocking me. His dick stiffened, the sore-covered tip peeking through a gray sheaf of foreskin. The sight was repulsive, an antithesis of everything I do on camera. I hated him on an atomic level.

The Rattler continued his monologue, pleasuring himself shamelessly.

"So, I've got your little toy. Well—she's *my* little toy, now. I sure hope you enjoy the show, Leon. It'll be the last time you see your bitch alive. Press record, and don't blink—I'd hate for you to miss a single second of this."

Stuart walked back out of frame, coming back moments later with Veronica slung over his shoulder. He tossed her roughly into the chair, restraining her. I pushed my craft to the highest speed allowed, staring at the tracker's progress. The city limits were behind me, the approximate location slowly tightening. My heart raced as I desperately hoped to reach her before it was too late.

Veronica's hair clung to her face in sweaty clumps, her eyes heavily lidded. She had clearly been sedated, her bottom lip swollen and dotted in dried blood. Her shirt and bra had been removed—another needling at my expense. The Rattler squeezed her cheeks, his slimy tongue running from chin to temple. He hissed, stroking himself and staring back to the camera.

161

"She tastes even better than I'd imagined. I wonder what her insides taste like? Oh—but you know. Don't you, Leon? You've explored this curvy brown body with your tongue extensively, I'd imagine," he growled. I screamed, punching the dash, hoping this waking nightmare would end. Stuart continued his vile taunting, his thin and diseased member erect.

"Well," he continued, "I've been waiting a long time to hurt this little thing. Now that I have her, it's showtime."

The Rattler backhanded Veronica across the jaw, her head whipping to the side while spittle and blood flew from her mouth. She awoke, crying in pain and mumbling. The panic in her eyes broke my heart—she was so scared, so alone in that awful place. My engine roared, the speed topped out as I rocketed towards the approximate area where she was being held.

"Fucking hurry up! Goddamn it!" I shouted, smashing my fist down on the dash. No matter how hard I raged, it would not make the trace go any faster. The hopelessness of my situation made my stomach churn. Stuart landed another cruel strike to Veronica's face, resulting in pained sobs.

"Good, she's awake," he hissed, "I don't want you to miss all the beautiful anguish I'm about to give you, Veronica. It'll go down in history."

"Fuck you! I did *nothing* to you!" she shouted, keeping a brave face. The Rattler laughed—the sound of dead leaves crumbling in a mausoleum. It wasn't the laugh of a human. He was far less.

"I'm fairly certain that a bee has never slighted a yellow-jacket. They simply feed on them. That's what I am, my sweet. A wasp among a world of worker bees. You go about your lives—plotting, grinning, complying. I wear a skin that fools your simple minds, and I strike when it's too late for you to do anything about it."

Without another word, Stuart walked off camera. I could hear the faint metallic clangs of him rifling through weapons and tools. Veronica sweated profusely, her face red and swollen. I'd have done anything to reach through the feed—to tell her it would all be okay. To tell her I loved her. He walked back, a rusty hacksaw in one hand, a blowtorch in the other.

My eyes darted to the trace again, the circle reduced to a ten-mile radius. It wasn't enough. I needed to stop the madness. No matter how hard I fought the urge, I couldn't look away. I didn't want to see her suffer, but I knew it was her last moments alive. Though it would haunt me, I loved her, and I couldn't bear the thought of not seeing her again. Every second of her life was precious to me, even if she was being torn apart.

Stuart set the blowtorch on the floor beside him, letting the teeth of the saw rest right above her kneecap. Veronica wept, unable to speak from the violent sobs racking her small form. He cruelly dragged the blade back and forth, blood welling while skin split. Pained screeches replaced my girl's cries. It was a sound I'd never be able to get out of my mind. His forceful hacking was cruel, muscle tissue gouging under the pressure of his relentless assault.

After a few more moments of sawing, Stuart hit the bone. The sickening sound of metal scraping Veronica's femur made me retch, bile spewing from my mouth onto my shirt. He laughed, applying more pressure until her leg severed completely. Blood gushed at an alarming rate while he lifted the blowtorch and ignited it. It was a sick parallel, a wave of torturous agony when the flame met bloodied and mangled muscle tissue.

The wet hiss of cauterizing flesh brought my mind back to Leah. That damned red room. This time was worse. It wasn't a child, but it was the only person I'd ever loved suffering before me. The radius had reduced to eight miles, but it wasn't enough. I screamed, my side throbbing as I pleaded to whatever God lies beyond the veil for a miracle. A miracle that would not come.

"That was fun *and* a workout!" The Rattler mocked, another gale of deathly chuckles spewing from his cracked and festered lips. Veronica only screamed, incapable of words. Her vocal cords already sounded raw and painful. He lifted the severed limb to his mouth with one hand, sniffing the fresh blood and masturbating.

"I've been longing for this," Stuart said before running his diseased tongue across the bloodied end. His face smeared, glistening under the dingy yellow light of his red room.

"Mmmmm, exquisite. Sadly, Veronica—I won't be able to give you the extensive treatment I planned for. Your little boyfriend is likely nearing us. Time is pressing." He dropped the limb, walking back off camera. Veronica's head slumped over—she had fainted from shock. My trace had reduced to a five-mile radius, ramshackle houses blurring by.

The Rattler called out to me over the feed as he pilfered for another tool to hurt her with.

"Leon—you've always been partial to your hammer, is that right? Me, I've always been one for my lovely insects and blades. For once, I think I'm going to do it your way. You've *inspired* me."

It was the last thing I needed to hear. The radius was down to two miles, and I was scanning for the hearse I'd seen him use before. Stuart came back on screen, his fingers twirling a claw

164

hammer by its handle. His smile was jagged, blood dripping from sharp teeth.

All of his theatricality dried up when Stuart brought the claw side of the hammer down into the soft flesh above her clavicle. Blood flew in a sick spray, and he pried it backwards, breaking bone and flaying part of her torso open. The Rattler withdrew the claw side from her wound, blood spewing down her chest. I wept as he brought the hammer down onto her relentlessly over and over. The first blow broke her jaw, making it appear to lean.

Veronica's screams skipped like a scratched record from the downpour of vicious blows. Bones snapped, bruises and massive welts forming all over her. He was relentless and merciless, giving her no reprieve from his cruelty. Each blow was random, but he never struck her in the same place twice. It was cold, calculated, and extremely effective.

Just as the address pinged on my tracker, Stuart dropped the hammer unceremoniously. He turned to face the camera head on, a proud smile on his gaunt face.

"Thanks, Leon. I wish I could give you more, but we both know that you're close. Until we meet again."

With that, The Rattler walked off screen and never returned. I screamed, pummeling the dash with my fists until they bled and the skin of my knuckles had flayed off. Veronica's head was bowed over, her tan skin black and red from the brutalizing she endured. Her breaths were small and shallow. There wasn't much time left.

Chapter XXVII: Farewell

I didn't even kill the car when I whipped onto Stuart's property. Adrenaline had bypassed my aches, the urgency of the situation all consuming. My vehicle was the only one in the yard—a clear sign that he'd already made his escape. I sprinted to the door, my pistol out and ready, just in case.

The front door swung open freely when I tried it. I gagged, the stench of the house overwhelming. Every surface was covered in human skin, some of which still appeared fresh. My strides quickened, and I tried each door on my way through. The third one I opened revealed a stairwell leading down. I didn't need to try any more doors—I knew I'd found where Veronica had been tortured.

My feet were heavy, my descent every bit literal and metaphorical. Some say ignorance is bliss. Those moments of dread made me inclined to agree. I couldn't leave Veronica in that place. I saw her when I reached the bottom, her beautiful hair frizzed and clumped in blood.

"Baby, I'm here!" I shouted, hastening to her. My girl. My

poor, sweet, beautiful girl. He had ruined her. I frantically unbound her, taking her into my arms. She was barely breathing, her body dented and mangled from the hammer wounds. I cradled her head and spoke softly to her.

"I'm so sorry. I tried to get here sooner, baby. I tried so fucking hard," I said between sobs, gently kissing her forehead. Her beautiful face had been misshapen, but she was still the prettiest woman I'd ever laid eyes on. Veronica's eyes slowly shifted beneath heavy lids, locking with mine. Although she was almost gone, she put her hands over mine and stroked them. Even at the end of it all, Veronica was my light. My comfort—the only one who could save me from myself.

"It's—it's not your fault, Leon," she said in a small and fading voice. I couldn't hold back the pain, crying harder, holding her close.

"Neither was what happened. You have to forgive yourself. No one else would bat an eye over how broken this world is. You're not evil, baby. I could never have fallen in love with you if you were."

Every word was a battle. Veronica grew colder by the second. I knew I had to make my next words count. She needed to know how much she meant to me.

"Veronica, you were the love of my life. You're my hero. I don't know how to do this without you here, baby. I love you so much."

"I love you, too. I'm sorry we couldn't spend more time together. But these weeks have been the happiest of my life."

I kissed Veronica, holding her against me tightly so she wouldn't be so cold when she went. My tears fell upon her, an ache in my heart unlike any I'd ever felt. Our lips did not part until she stopped breathing. For a time—I couldn't say whether hours or minutes—I held the only person who ever loved me for who I truly was. I wept, and cursed a world that would give me something so good and then take it away.

When my senses finally returned, I rose with Veronica in my arms. We ascended the stairs, her head on my shoulder. I'd miss the way her hair smelled, the way she nuzzled against me when we'd read together. Nothing would ever be the same.

I morosely carried the woman who gave me everything when I thought all was lost. Now, it truly was. I walked out the front door and eased her onto the backseat. Before I left, there was one thing I had to do—burn down The Rattler's den.

With numb fingers, I pulled a jerry can from the trunk and a box of matches. I trudged through the dank confines of Stuart's home, dousing the walls. He'd have to start over, cold comfort in the colossal fallout I was facing. With one last look, I struck a match and set the house ablaze. Purifying fire baptized the walls, the skin blackening and curling at the edges.

When I finally got back into my hover car, the sound system squawked frantically. Asimov had been calling me for over ten minutes. In all the chaos, my earpiece had fallen out before I went inside. I panicked, hitting accept.

"Asy, what's wrong?"

"Sir, there is a militia sieging the property. They haven't reached the door yet, but it doesn't look good."

"How many? Were you able to get a count?"

"A rough one, yes, sir. There are close to three hundred hostiles."

I slammed into drive and sped towards Crimson Manor as we spoke.

"Okay. Asimov, the most important thing you can do is keep Allen safe. I don't give a damn about anything but that. Do you understand?"

"Yes, sir. I understand."

"Good. Be ready to lie down fire. Activate the turrets and proximity mines on the exits. I'm thirty minutes out. Please be careful."

"I will protect Master Allen at all costs, sir."

My head felt numb, the speedometer topped out. I couldn't lose Allen, too. I'd go to Hell with a smile before I let that happen. The miles flew by, my knuckles raw and aching from the death-grip I had on the steering wheel. Despite my crushed hope, there was still something to fight for. I drove on, headed towards a future unknown and ever uncertain.

Chapter XXVIII: Moving Up In the World

Richard Vostares sat at a table in Cantina Molestas, his favorite lunchtime spot on Vostares Island. He ran a hand through his thinning black hair, stubble showing on his grizzled face. The past month or so had been taxing, to say the least. With Spiritcrusher identified and pinned to the ops center attacks, he finally had one less problem on his plate. Shame it had to be dealt with on vacation, but that was the price of being the boss.

His eyes rolled back to whites, a low growl in his throat. Richard shivered, then resumed eating his steak. A moment later, a small boy (Rich would guess around seven, but who's counting?) rose from under the table, wiping his mouth with the back of his hand. Richard nodded gruffly at him, shooing him away with a quick hand wave.

It was always easier to make business decisions after a good nut. Richard smiled, pulling a phone from his beige board shorts. He clicked Stuart's name on his contact list. After a few rings, the familiar voice of his favorite killer responded.

"Good evening, Richard."

"Good evening, Stuart. How'd your little date go? Get your dick wet?" he said, guffawing and slapping the top of the glossy table over his own wit. His response was met with silence. After a moment, he said, "This fucking thing working? You there, Stu?"

"Yeah, I'm here."

Fucking asshole. It was a good joke. I thought serial killers would be more funny.

"Well? How'd it go, asshole?" Richard asked, keeping a playful tone in his voice. Even though The Rattler freaked him the fuck out, he'd never let it show. Perceived weakness was a liability he'd not allow.

"It went—fine. I'd have loved to take my time with her, but—"

"Spiritcrusher?"

"Yeah. Downside of doing it live. Even so, it worked. And my hunger is sated. For now."

Creepy motherfucker.

"Well, that's good, at least. Keep me updated on the assault if you hear something before I do."

"Will do, Rich," The Rattler said.

"Oh, one more thing. Before you disappear again."

"Yes?"

"I've spoken to the PCP board members. Your initiative is being rewarded. Expect a fatter deposit going forwards."

"How much fatter are we talking, here?"

Richard grimaced, his brown eyes rolling. Not a 'thank you' or anything out of this guy. At times, dealing with psychos almost made him want to get back into a legitimate industry. He never would, though, of course. Legitimate industry frowned upon getting lunchtime blowjobs from children or anything else that he deemed fun. Not worth the hassle. Psychos it was.

"Forty percent. Congratulations," Rich said, scratching his balls under his shorts with his free hand.

"Thank you. It'll help with my new den," Stuart said, the tone of his voice verging on hostile or resentful. Richard knew why—the crazy cunt was worried about his goddamn skins. To each their own, he supposed. A child's ass was how he got off, but not everyone was built that way. Regardless, the attitude pissed him off.

Forty percent was a *huge* fucking pay increase. Ingrates and psychos. What a pain in the ass. The Rattler was both, apparently. Fantastic.

"Yeah, it will. Your contribution is highly appreciated and valued. Bye, Stuart."

"Bye, Richard."

The call ended, and Rich finished his meal. He took a healthy glug of beer, patting his full belly with a free hand. After a considerably meaty belch, Richard rose and casually strode towards the office. There was another board meeting in a half hour. He had just enough time to get into a suit and tie and fix his hair. Boss or not, it wouldn't do to look like a fucking beach bum.

* * *

The first hour was a deluge of bureaucratic bullshit. Spreadsheets, graphs, the whole kit and kaboodle. Richard struggled to stay awake through the compulsory death by presentation

172

inherent to corporate meetings. Once nerd-boy finally stopped yammering, it was time to get to brass tacks.

He rose from his seat at the head of the massive oak table and cleared his throat to get everyone's attention. It didn't take long for them to oblige.

"Good afternoon, everyone. While our margins look good *now*, I'm sure you're all aware that things are not well. With Atlanta out of commission, we have no product to sell. Aside from home tapes amongst ourselves, everything was in that server farm. Everything. As much as it pains me to admit it, that masked fuck really put a kink in our works. Not to mention the one on the Eastern coast who's been stirring up trouble."

The expressions around Rich were appropriately somber for his remarks. If they were upset *now*, he wasn't looking forward to how they'd react to his next words.

"So—we have to cut back. We need to reduce our staff by at least thirty percent. Given my projections, it's mandatory. It'll take a solid year to build up another content base. Without the cuts, that would bankrupt us in four months."

Dismayed murmurs and gasps broke out, the board members frantic. Lisa Devram spoke up, asking a question the rest likely wanted to.

"How can we keep over a thousand employees quiet about our organization? A disgruntled employee is a big enough problem for a normal company. What do we do when one or all of them attempt to blackmail us?"

Richard smiled, feeling his testosterone surge. He had been looking forward to this part of the meeting all day. It was rare to get an 'action movie' moment in his position anymore. Life at the top was luxurious, but incredibly dry in action.

"Well, allow me to demonstrate," Rich said, grinning as he pulled a revolver from his coat pocket. He fired at Lisa, the bullet ripping through her eye and blowing out the back of her skull. Brains and blood slid wetly down the leather office chair as she slumped forwards. Before the other board members could react, he fired into two more skulls. Thirty percent of his board was three—the numbers didn't lie.

Once it was clear that he'd finished capping suits, the rest of the members stopped shrieking like little girls. Richard realized his cock was rock hard. It felt good to pull the trigger, from time to time.

"Okay? Everyone on board with the plan?" he asked, leering at them madly. They nodded, their weak chins quivering. Richard smiled, snapping his fingers.

"Right, good then! Now, on to another matter: What would you like for dinner? The choices are Thai or Mexican."

His question was met with dumbfounded silence. Eventually, he got the retards to raise their hands and vote. Thai, it was. He'd always been partial to Thai. Maybe it was that college trip to Bangkok. Who knew?

"Great, Thai sounds outstanding." Richard paged his assistant on the intercom.

"Lily, send up the Thai, please."

"Yes, sir. Is there anything else you need?"

"No, that'll be all. Thanks, sugar tits."

"Oh—you're welcome, sir."

Minutes later, a light knock came at the boardroom door. Richard grinned, his appetite roaring after blowing some brains out.

"Come in!" he said gleefully.

Seven Thai children filed through the doorway, nude and

shivering. An armed guard marched them through and lined them up at gunpoint. Fuck, he loved Thai. The board stripped their clothing off. It was time to end the meeting on a bang.

Chapter XXIX: In Transit

Although I was tempted to keep Asimov on the line, I knew it wouldn't help. The span from my location to Crimson Manor felt infinite and utterly unreachable. Tree clusters zoomed by, the poor gawking at me as I flew by at over two hundred miles per hour. Inside the craft, it was silent. I couldn't help but look back at Veronica's still form.

It was cruel. Why couldn't I have more time? Why couldn't I hold on to some small sliver of light? Hadn't I earned it? Had I not suffered enough?

No matter my objections, fate's cruel blade severed my last strand of hope for a happy life. Rage seethed and boiled, my melancholic sorrow fuel for the maelstrom of flames brewing inside. All I could focus on was reaching home. The front would be a foolhardy route, knowing the large opposition was likely staged there. Thankfully, I implemented a contingency for that exact circumstance. I needed to get in, arm up, and wipe those PCP cunts off the face of the earth.

Vurisberg limits came into view—a whole new set of problems laid at my feet. People fought in the streets, destroying any shop not yet ruined from the riot prior. Bricks flew, some shattering glass, some faces. Violence hung heavily in the filthy air, the roar of angry cries filling my ears. It only stirred my building rage to dizzying new heights.

The road was blocked by people fighting, some of whom turned and eyed my vehicle meaningfully. In my panicked departure, I'd chosen the Lamborghini Z-666—a hovercraft with a market value of five point seven million dollars. Although I had no way of anticipating a riot, the folly of using such a desirable vehicle dawned on me. The group of rioters shifted focus to me, some people halting mid fist fight for a gander. When a brick flew at the windshield, I knew things were going to get out of hand quickly if I didn't move.

I have never claimed to be a hero. I'm certainly no saint, nor pious, nor forgiving. My decision wasn't an easy one, but the fact of the matter was quite simple: I'd kill a million strangers to save Allen. I shifted back to drive, engaging the overdrive thrusters. The mob converged, less than ten meters away. "Either you or Allen. Get fucked," I growled, slamming the accelerator down.

Some rioters were smart enough to get out of my way. Others—not so much. I screamed gleefully as people bent and broke against the tungsten hood, their blood spattering and teeth flying. In my rearview, I watched, enraptured at the sight of people on fire from the rear thrusters. It was beautiful.

Bodies crumpled from the force applied by my high-speed battering ram. If they didn't want to make a hole, I was quite content with creating one, myself. Each head bouncing off the grill gave me something to enjoy on my way to Hell. No life was sacred if it put itself between me and my destination. The world could fucking burn, for all I cared.

I roared, unrepentant primal rage rattling my chest and making my vision blur and redden. The blockage lessened once I got through the main strip, but it would not be an easy ride. My route would take me through Southside, where the violence would undoubtedly double or even triple compared to what I was already contending with. Although they'd never been necessary before, I was grateful for the installed turret resting beneath the hood. I turned right, my eyes scanning the chaos.

Just as expected, Southside was a war-zone. Guns fired in every direction, muzzles flaring and shots echoing off the concrete buildings. The main point of contention became apparent quickly. There was a gang war actively happening. One side wore green outfits, the other black clothes and red cloth masks. A memory of a time that seemed so long ago came flooding back to me. It was the same gang who'd attempted to rob me and rape Veronica on our first date.

I engaged a toggle on my dash, the .50 caliber barrel rising from its hidden compartment beneath the hood. With a few quick keystrokes on the display, I specified targets based on clothing. Those stupid fucks were going to get a taste of their own medicine—being outgunned and overpowered. The barrel spun up to speed, a notification alerting me when the weapon system was live.

I pressed the fire button as I rolled through, laughing at the chaos unfolding. My body vibrated from the rapid fire assault, the gunshots deafening and thunderous. Each round found a home inside of a scumbag's chest cavity. Their torsos exploded into a fine red mist, organs flying from massive exit wounds in slimy chunks. Bodies slumped, the swarm of rioters scattering at the fierce roar of high caliber death.

Something had snapped inside of me. I felt my fingers going back to the control parameters. It was as though my autopilot had engaged. My targeting parameters shifted from one gang to everyone holding a weapon. I had been lenient before, a mistake I'd never make again. Criminals were criminals. Who knew how many of these motherless fucks were affiliated with PCP, anyway? I pressed fire again, watching the barrel fire without prejudice into the writhing mass surrounding me.

If my identity was blown, who fucking cared about discretion? Heads exploded into meaty pulp, limbs ripped off as the hail of bullets slalomed side-to-side. It was a gun, but it had the effects of taking a hot saw to bodies—shredding and ruining. No medical center in the world could undo the gangland genocide I was executing. Fuck them all. Fuck everyone who could walk through life comfortably by taking from those who'd earned their keep.

My throat was raw, my scream unending. It was a true berserk, all of my hurt redirected into a vicious killing spree. By the time I rolled through the last block of contested turf, the streets and sidewalks were littered with corpses. The gutters ran red that night. Scurrying rodents amongst the dank labyrinthian sewers would gorge on the flesh and blood of the executed.

I had five miles between myself and the secret entrance. Luckily, rioters dwindled by the time the turret ran dry on ammunition. None of the carnage made me feel better, but I had no regrets. If I survived the day, the world would face a newer, meaner Spiritcrusher. They would not be prepared.

The entrance came up on my left. To any passersby, it looked like a derelict car wash—a relic of times long gone.

A time where food wasn't scarce and gangs and pedophiles hadn't strong armed law enforcement into submission. I pulled into the bay, where the steel shutters automatically lowered. The chamber hissed from pressurization, my vehicle slowly lowering on a hydraulic lift. I was underground now, in a dark tunnel I hoped I'd never need to use.

The headlights of my craft reflected and danced off the concrete, my speed increasing. My heart pounded from the urgency of the situation. The Lamborghini's engine roared, echoing through the dark passage like a beast rising from the depths. I tried paging Asimov, and let out a loud curse. There was simply too much concrete encasing me. Communications couldn't be established until I reached the topside again.

In the darkness, I let my thoughts run wild. There was nothing else to do, and I couldn't stop my racing mind. I loved Veronica, and I loved Allen. Nothing else mattered. If I failed saving him—I was going to end it all. Those thoughts weren't a recent phenomenon, but in the face of all I'd endured, nothing else made sense. What is a life without someone beside you? Nothing.

I drove on, my knuckles scabbed and aching. My teeth clenched, my temples throbbing. Crimson Manor was two miles out. The pressure of the situation stabbed my chest in aching waves. It felt like I was having a heart attack.

The moment I saw a red glow, I slowed the craft. I controlled my urge to panic, driving up the ramp and mentally steeling myself for the ensuing bloodbath. At the end of the ramp, I drove onto another lift. Within a minute, I was in Crimson Manor, in a chamber directly beneath the armory. Underground, I couldn't hear any gunfire, but I knew that meant nothing. Hope is a cruel and treacherous thing.

My aching side pained me as I got out of the vehicle and walked over to a sealed door. I input the security code into a number pad beside it, entering the elevator once it opened. On the way up, I let my darkness take over. There was no time for mercy or hesitation. The elevator door opened, and I stepped out quickly into the armory.

I changed into my gear as quickly as I could, my breathing erratic. After grabbing a black duffel from a table near the door, I shoveled every filled barrel magazine I had into it. I grabbed my AA-12, slinging it and inserting a mag. The chunk of a shell chambering soothed me. It was the calm before the storm. With one last look back, I kicked the door open, my weapon at high-ready.

Chapter XXX: All Or Nothing

The hallways were quiet as I made my way towards the foyer. I paged Asy, and let out a huge sigh of relief at his instant response.

"Yes, sir. Asimov reporting."

"I'm here. Is Allen okay?"

"Yes, sir. He is in the control room providing locations and real-time updates. The turrets are active, as well as all the explosives."

"Fantastic. Okay, Asy. All we can do is keep calm and shoot them when they get through. Sadly, there's no 'if' to this situation. As prepared as I was, I never expected an attack from a force this size."

"That's not your fault, sir. When you fight the devil, there's always a risk."

"Damn straight. I'll see you soon," I said, ending the call. Asimov stood at the base of the grand staircase, his weapon systems out and ready for action. I directed us to firing positions on either side of the foyer, activating the firing covers he had placed in preparation. The small metal devices whirred, shifting until they had configured themselves.

I let the barrel of my shotgun rest in the firing port, my eyes scanning for movement through the bulletproof visor. Crimson Manor's side exits would be impassible if anyone triggered the bombs. That made the front door a hot spot for combat. My finger rested parallel to the trigger guard, my selector switch already on fire.

"Leon, you there?" Allen asked over comms. His voice was shaky, but not to the degree I'd have expected. Training had hardened the young man. Even with the dogs of war at our doorstep, I couldn't help but feel proud.

"Yeah, Al. I'm here," I said.

"Did—did you make it in time?"

"No. I tried, kid. I really did. I just wasn't fast enough."

Sadness overtook his voice at my news. I heard faint sniffles and sobs on the other end. After a minute or so, he spoke again.

"It's not your fault, Leon. I'm sorry, too. We both loved her."

"Yes we did. Let's not let her death be in vain, kid. Let's give these pieces of shit hell. Are you ready?"

"I'm ready. So far, the turrets have dropped twenty contacts. It looks like they're planning what to do next."

"Okay, that's good. It buys us time. Activate Spiritwing and set it to code red defense. That should even the odds a bit more."

"Roger, Wilco."

I listened intently over the next few minutes for the sounds of gunfire. Each second felt like an eternity, and I began worrying that Al may have not activated Spiritwing. Those concerns instantly halted when a series of explosions boomed in the distance.

"Two vehicles down, contacts scrambling," Allen said. I nodded in grim satisfaction. Money never brought me happiness. It never held my hand or kept me company, but I was grateful it could buy me bullets. In the end, they brought me joy more often than high dollar whores or bags of narcotics. Gunfire rattled off, Spiritwing laying into the ground troops outside.

I kept my eyes forward, the muzzle flare of distant gunfire illuminating the growing darkness. Distance was hard to gauge, but it was easy to see the small army growing larger, closer. Spiritwing could only do so much before they grew too close. The turrets atop Crimson Manor rattled off gunfire above us, the hostiles within firing range. Allen came back over comms.

"Leon, one guy is holding something. It doesn't look like a normal gun. I can't quite make out what it is."

"Can you describe it to me?"

"It's a long tube," Al said, sounding unsure of himself. My eyes widened at the description. In the distance, a massive boom rang out. I didn't need Allen to tell me what happened—Spiritwing rocketed towards us, the helicopter a crumpled boulder of melting steel. When it collided with the roof, I could feel the ground vibrating beneath me.

"Leon, our rooftop turrets are out of commission. They're advancing. Two smaller groups are taking flank positions."

"That's fine. Let them get blown up. Al, no matter what happens. No matter what you hear—don't leave the control room. It's the safest place for you. Do you understand?" I asked loudly, feeling my adrenaline kicking up.

"I understand."

"Good. I love you, Allen. I promise to do everything I can to keep you safe."

"I do. I love you, too, Dad."

Tears streamed my face beneath the mask, my finger easing into the trigger guard. The main body of the army halted a distance away. I knew they were waiting on their flankers to do the job. A few minutes later, explosions rang out from both the east and west wings. They were going to have to earn my kill. It'd be a cold day in Hell before I went down easy.

"Asy, give them all you've got when they cross the threshold. It's all or nothing, now," I said, eyeing the slowly advancing swarm of gunmen. Asimov looked over and nodded. His barrels rotated, ready for rapid fire in an instant.

"Yes, Master Leon. No mercy, no surrender. Whether we stand or fall, it has been an honor fighting the good fight, sir."

"Likewise, my friend. Let's not plan for failure, though. We've made it through worse than this."

"Leon, they're advancing. Contact imminent," Allen said, his voice rising in pitch. Men in gray fatigues came into view, their M-16s punching dents into the bulletproof glass. I hunkered down low beneath my cover, preparing a concussion grenade for their breach. Their pointman kneeled before the door, placing a charge. The air was thick with tension, my gut rolling in sickly anticipation.

My ears rang violently as the door flew by me. It slammed into a wall with enough force to flatten a man. I pulled a pin on the grenade I'd been nursing and rolled it to their feet while hunkering down. The PCP operatives didn't notice it as they poured inside, well over thirty men in its proximity. A light blue light flashed, the crowd of advancing men falling to their backs and screaming in pain. Without a word, Asimov fired into the downed combatants with accurate and lightning fast shots. Blood pooled beneath their twitching corpses, shell casings jingling across the freshly waxed marble floor. I didn't even have time to fire a single shot.

Our enemy did not hesitate to flood more men towards the door, their shots wildly inaccurate but overwhelmingly plentiful. I pulled the trigger, walking my shots side-to-side as the men sprinted inside. Their eyes widened as death took them. Each magazine change was a reassurance that the army dwindled. The air roiled with the sweet scents of gunpowder and blood. Bullets plinked off of my cover, some shots flying well overhead as gunmen still pulling their triggers fell back into a bloody heap.

Every wave got a little closer to us, my healing wound aching and eyes stinging from sweat. Allen's count had dropped to the one hundred mark, but I felt fatigue creeping in. In all the confusion and chaos, Al didn't notice the flame troopers on either side of the home, taking a flamethrower to the last tangible reminder of my parents' legacy. We battled on, smoke swirling around us. Each shot was a kill. By the time we cleared the frontal assault, Crimson Manor was up in flames.

Asimov and I ran through the doorway, scanning our sectors for remaining PCP grunts. We each dropped the flame troopers still actively at work on my home. The fire systems fought against the flames valiantly, but by the time it was over, half of the house my father built was reduced to a smoldering ruin.

Chapter XXXI: Exodus

Allen packed away the last of his belongings into a black travel case. His eyes were darkly ringed. Neither of us had slept. It was five in the morning, and we were about to leave the only home I'd ever known. Asimov had been tirelessly packing my armory and mission essential equipment into an armored hover van since we'd repelled the PCP assault. It was only a matter of time before the bastards realized their plan failed. We'd be long gone before then.

Before we left, there was one matter left to address. Allen tossed his case alongside mine on the backseat floorboard of the van. We looked one another in the eye and nodded. It was time.

Asimov pulled up in the Ferrari, killing the engine and opening the rear passenger door. He gingerly lifted Veronica from the backseat where she lay, her hair cascading over his sleek metallic arm. I directed him to the grave I'd dug. It was in the center of our now ruined garden, a spot my mother often daydreamed. Something told me she and Veronica would have gotten along.

Asy lowered her into the ground, and we all bowed our heads in silence. I felt tears flowing, and didn't control them. If I was going to be a father to Allen, he needed to see that strong men cry. I needed to show him a better path than the one I'd walked for so long. This was one step in the right direction.

Once I felt able to speak, I cleared my throat as I gazed upon Veronica one last time.

"Veronica was a beautiful soul. She gave kindness and love without ever expecting anything in return. Until the moment she died, she spent every second taking care of me. I never felt worthy of love before her. I do now, and I owe it to her. I owe everything to her. She saved my life, and she will be missed."

My voice cracked with a fresh flood of tears. Allen began speaking next, his eyes red and bleary.

"Veronica showed me what a mother looked like, even if she didn't know it. When you were stuck in bed, she'd make me eat and brush my hair. She read to me every night until you could get up again. I'll always remember that. I don't remember my actual mom, but I will never forget Veronica. I loved her."

I wept and took Allen under my arm. We held one another and let the pain and tears run their course as Asimov gently covered her with soil. Once her funeral was over, we had to go. I sat in the passenger seat, letting Asy drive. My nerves were too shot to do it myself. The charred remains of Crimson Manor shrank in the rearview.

There were rumors of another vigilante like me on the east coast. It was a long shot, but I needed all the help I could get. We had lost too much to throw in the towel on our war. Children just like Allen were waiting for a savior to come and unshackle them from the demons holding them captive.

To love and lose is an agony I thought I'd never experience again. Wherever I went, Veronica would be with me. In my heart, guiding me. In my mind, keeping the darkness at bay. She cured me, and it cost her everything. I'd never let that sacrifice be in vain.

The world cannot be cruel unless allowed by uncaring people. For every evil deed, there is a pair of eyes intentionally looking away. With Allen at my side, we would turn the tides on those who prey upon children. Revenge for my love was my driving force—a fire inextinguishable. The Rattler would die by my hands. Richard Vostares would finally atone for creating the monster I became.

When all seems lost, love will shine a light on the good that lingers. For every ounce of pain, there is a lesson to strengthen the soul. I am no hero—just a broken man too stubborn to forgive that which is unforgivable. The world was asleep to its cancer, something I'd fix. Harming the innocent is a crime that cannot go unanswered.

No pedophile will draw breath without shuddering in fear at the mention of my name. No child will go to sleep hoping not to wake. Every wrong will be brought to light. Vengeance is coming.

I am Spiritcrusher, and this is my crusade.

Afterword

Hey—you've made it. For a while, I wasn't certain I'd be able to finish writing this book. Life has a funny way of curb stomping your nuts, sometimes. Luckily, people are resilient beings.

This book will be a time capsule for me, one day. A point in time that I can point to and measure my progress with as an author and person. I love Splatterpunk—but like all other areas where social interaction occurs—people can be snakes. Despite the back-biting and falsities, I remain standing.

I make a promise to you, my reader, here and now—this trilogy will conclude before 2025. I have other projects for you to look forward to in the meantime, including a Splatter-Fantasy novel that's underway. After diving head-first into my personal trauma for roughly 50,000 words, ya boy needs a fucking break from pedophiles. Just remember—a break doesn't mean forever.

So—thank you. Without readers, these books would be inert bricks with no meaning. Words will never express my gratitude to each of you who support me and other indie authors in the scene. We open our veins onto the page, and you lap it up without hesitation. It makes me proud to be a small part of the extreme movement.

Ever onward and upward, my friends.

—James Fisher

Made in the USA
Columbia, SC
11 December 2024

47733056R00121